REBUILDING HOME

Rebuilding Home

MORGAN MENEFEE

Kraken Cup Media

This novel is entirely a work of fiction. The names, characters, and incidents portrayed in it are the work of the author's imagination. Any resemblance to actual persons, living or dead, events, or localities is entirely coincidental.

Copyright © 2022 by Morgan Menefee

All rights reserved. No part of this book may be reproduced in any manner whatsoever without written permission except in the case of brief quotations embodied in critical articles and reviews.

First Printing, 2022

Library of Congress Control Number: 2022909638
ISBN 979-8-218-00824-6 (paperback)

This book is the result of the influence of more people than I can adequately thank here, but I will try. This book is for:
> ~my family, who taught me to dream.
> ~my best friend, who allows me to be strong and independent with him.
> ~Mr. Ross, who told me to write.
> ~Dr. Tafoya, who makes me question every punctuation mark.
> ~the God who imbued me with this passion.
> ~the sense of humor that prompted me to put Dr. Tafoya and God next to each other.

~ 1 ~

Dani pulled herself up out of her little car. She tugged the hem of her t-shirt down, shamefully aware of her muffin top and the dig of her jeans into her waist. Thankfully, there was no welcoming party waiting, though she wouldn't be surprised if her mother was watching from the kitchen window. She glanced up at the gathering thunderheads and hoped the storm would make it here. The cracks in the ground cried for rain, and the humidity was suffocating. Sucking in a deep breath of hot, sticky air, Dani swung the back door open to grab her bag. Time to face her new start.

Somehow, the air inside the house was easier to breathe. Her mother must have on every fan in the house to achieve that. Dani kicked off her shoes in the mudroom and stepped into the kitchen. She found herself face to face with her own mirror image, if she'd lost 50 pounds and gotten a deep farmer's tan.

"Hi, Mama," she dropped her bag and accepted her mother's tight embrace.

"Is that all you brought?"

"There's more in the car. I'll get it later."

"Okay. Well, I just got your cabinets cleaned out and some dishes put in them. You can rearrange however you want. There's some sandwich stuff in the fridge, but you can eat with us whenever you want." Dani trailed after her through an empty dining room and into the living room. "Grandma had an extra couch and TV. It's not much, but you can make it your own."

"Thanks, Mom. It's fine." In truth, the charity made her uncomfortable, and she was sure there was more coming.

"There's a full-size bed upstairs, but we didn't put the frame together. Figured you'd want to pick your bedroom. I can help you with it now if you want."

"No, I'll get it later. Thank you so much." Mama looked about to object, a hint of a frown crossing her face, but only for a moment.

"The rest of the downstairs is a mess. Some storage, some spots where repairs need done, but it's functional for now."

"Sounds good. What chores need done down here?" Coming home to start over meant going back to her farm-girl roots. Dani hoped it would be like riding a bicycle.

"I wrote them all down for you." Mama went back to the kitchen and Dani followed, spotting a half-sheet of paper covered in her mother's neat handwriting. "Just calves in the pen off the dairy barn, a couple boars in the hoop barn, and the finishing barn is full." Dani nodded, skimming the list. Easy enough. Throw some feed, fill some water troughs, and make sure nothing died.

"Got it." *Now what?*

"You want me to help you carry stuff in and get set up? I've got a little time before I need to go cool hogs off again."

"No, I think I'll leave that 'til it's cooler. I might go see the calves and check out the old barn now. I can't believe it's still standing."

"Just barely. Be careful. We need to pull it down. I'll see you at supper?" Dani nodded and followed Mama out to her car. "I'm glad you're here. The house needs lived in," Mama said and pulled her door shut. Dani figured that's as close as they'd ever get to talking about why she was here.

She watched Mama pull out of the drive, then ambled toward the dairy barn. The calves flicked their ears and watched her approach, trying to decide if she was bringing food. They backed away as she reached the gate. Dani draped her arms over the gate and studied her new neighbors. Seven calves, all shades of brown and all skittish, but one with a dark spot on his nose was braver than the others. He took a tentative step closer, neck stretched long and low, sniffing in Dani's direction.

"I'll bring treats next time, guys." Dani pushed off the gate, scattering the calves. Sweat rolled down her back and made her shirt stick to her. Time to go take things inside. At least that would give her a break from the heat and humidity. She hefted a bag off her back seat onto her shoulder and grabbed the handles of another. She could feel the temperature difference as soon as she swung the back door open. Sweet relief.

Her phone buzzed in her back pocket and Dani took the excuse to drop the heavy bags to the kitchen floor. She pulled her phone from her back pocket and leaned against the fridge. Kat had messaged to see if she'd made it okay.

"Yup. Back to the land of no a/c. Maybe I'll finally lose some weight," she typed in response. She checked for any other messages, but there was nothing. Sliding the phone back into her pocket, Dani straightened. There was a bed to assemble and a few things to unpack before chore time.

Upstairs, Dani surveyed her bedroom options. The biggest room at the far end was out. Plaster was falling from the ceiling and she made a mental note to ask Papa if the roof had been repaired when she went up for supper. The next room wasn't bad, and it was conveniently located across from the bathroom, but it was half-filled with boxes. Dani moved on, hoping for a more move-in ready option. Side-stepping the bed frame and mattress propped against the hallway wall, Dani made her way into one of the two rooms at the end of the hall. It felt cooler than its neighbor, tempting, but the carpet was in tatters. Still, if the last room wasn't any better, it would do. The last room was the cleanest by far, with a bare wooden floor. It would need some elbow grease, but less than the room with the torn up carpet. Home sweet home. She drug the headboard in and paused. Across from the door was a window and a closet built out into the corner. If she put the headboard against the window so she could face the door, her only way in and out of bed would be crawling over the foot board. She'd be trapped. The only other option was to put the headboard on the same wall as the door. Not ideal, but better than being trapped.

Ten sweaty minutes and one newly forming bruise later, Dani's bed was assembled. It was a double bed, so her queen sheets would be a little big, but it would work. She wouldn't be spending much time here anyway. She'd spotted a beat up dresser in the room with the tattered carpet and drug it across the hall. It wasn't perfect, but it would do. She glanced at her phone. 5:47. There was time to make the bed and haul the bags upstairs before chores.

Back downstairs, Dani opened the purple duffel and pulled out the heavy plastic bottle. The Canadian whiskey probably tasted like lighter fluid, but it was cheap and the bottle was big enough to last a little while. A thump sounded upstairs as she set the bottle on the counter. Dani froze, heart racing as the irrational fear that she'd been found darted around her head.

"It's just plaster falling. No one can get here without being heard," she said aloud. Still, she carried only one bag of clothes up the stairs, keeping her other hand free, just in case. But no one was upstairs. Of course. She was being ridiculous.

All three bags upstairs, Dani slipped into the muck boots Mama had left by the back door. She counted the calves - all there - and tossed some grain into their trough. Next, she needed to carry water to the boars. She filled two five-gallon buckets about half-full at the hydrant. A bucket in each hand, she set off for the hoop barn. *When did it get so far away? Have buckets of water always been this heavy?* They'd certainly felt lighter when she was seventeen. Her farm muscles were definitely out of practice. She paused to rest twice on the way there, and her hands were definitely going to blister, but she made it. She watched the boars splash around in the water she poured them for a few minutes, catching her breath. Just the finishing barn to check, and they really shouldn't need anything. Dani gathered her buckets and headed that way. The din of the finishing floor, each pen containing pigs of roughly the same size waiting their turn for market, was the one thing she hadn't missed about the farm.

Bracing herself for the increase in volume, Dani lifted the latch and pulled the finishing barn door open. A pig squealed and trotted away from her down the narrow alley that ran in front of the pens.

"What the . . ." Dani turned the latch to secure the door behind her. "What pen do you belong in?" She scanned the pens, hoping it would be obvious where the thin white gilt belonged. No such luck. "Alright, best guess it is." She pulled out the rod holding the second pen closed and swung its gate open all the way across the alley, blocking the escaped pig from getting past the intended pen. And blocking herself out of the alley where she needed to be in order to drive the pig back in. She sighed and lifted her leg over the gate. The metal dug into the back of her thigh as she swung her other leg over. She dropped into the midst of the gilt's pen mates, who were flooding into the alley to see what was going on. She walked with them to the end of the alley and wedged her legs in front of the pigs, pushing with her knees while hissing and waving her arms. She'd feel this in the morning, but it was working. "Come on, let's go. Back in your pen." The pigs complied and she soon had the gate shut. She watched for a few minutes, but the pigs showed no signs of fighting the little gilt. She must have guessed right. That problem solved, Dani refocused on checking feeders. Everybody had plenty, so she glanced one more time at the gilt, saw she was rooting at the gate, unperturbed, and headed back toward the house.

Dani dropped the buckets by the water hydrant and stopped to survey her new, though probably temporary, home. It was beautiful, even if it did need love. True, the old barn behind the house leaned at a pretty severe angle, but the old rock and cinder block dairy barn was stunning in its own way. The house needed a coat of paint and some weeds trimmed, but that was doable. As she contemplated house colors - slate blue with dark wood shutters would be pretty - she caught movement in an upstairs window. Her heartbeat quickened. *Curtains? No. That was the biggest bedroom. No curtains there.*

"No one is here," but Dani wasn't convinced by her own assurances. "Probably just falling plaster." She heard a faint rumble and looked up. The thunderhead she'd admired earlier was now overhead. Intruder or no, she'd have to go inside or get wet soon. Stalling, Dani pulled out her phone and messaged Kat. Also a farm girl, Kat would appreciate her chore experiences. She was feeling better after a few messages with Kat, though she hadn't mentioned her fears of being found. The rumbles of thunder were growing more frequent, and the wind had picked up. Rain was coming.

Fears at least temporarily quashed, Dani started toward the house, taking care not to look at the windows. Inside, she kicked off her boots and checked to see if Mama had stocked the downstairs bathroom, just off the mud room, with towels and soaps. She found the bathroom cabinet stuffed with towels, wash cloths, and one bottle each of shampoo, conditioner, and body wash. *Thank God.* The upstairs bathroom needed a partial renovation and a good cleaning before she'd shower there. She darted upstairs to her room and grabbed a change of clothes. No bogeyman grabbed her, but still, she was relieved to be back on the ground floor.

Dani hated showers. She had ever since he took their peace and comfort from her. But she had to admit, it felt good to rinse the sweat away. Still, she rushed through, refusing to close her eyes. When she stepped out, a cool breeze through the bathroom window chilled her. She ruffled her hair dry and pulled on clean clothes. She kicked into her flip flops, grabbed her phone, and headed for the car.

It was sprinkling by the time Dani made it to her parents' home, just a mile away. Maybe, on nicer days, she'd walk. Papa was in his chair in the living room, flipping through *Farm Talk*. She gave him a quick peck on the cheek and wandered to the kitchen to help Mama finish getting supper on.

"You get the house all set up?" Papa asked between bites of meatloaf after an awkward prayer during which Dani felt uncertain whether to hold her parents' outstretched hands or fold her own together. Her faith, she realized, had suffered during her marriage as much as she had.

"The bed is up, but I haven't done much else to it yet. Gilt was out in the finishing barn, so chores took longer than I thought."

"Real thin one?" Dani nodded, mouth full of cheesy potatoes. "She does that. Squeezes through by the feeder, I think."

"She go in the second pen?"

"Yup. Sounds like you got it handled."

They finished supper in silence. Only the sounds of the storm accompanied their thoughts. It was a gentle rain, but Dani's head whipped toward the window at a bright flash of lightning.

"Hey, Papa, is the roof on that house good? I noticed plaster falling upstairs."

"Yeah, we fixed the roof a few years back, but not the inside. It'll take a lot of work if you decide to stay."

If I decide to stay, Dani echoed in her mind. *Where else would I go?* Her phone buzzed. Probably Kat wanting to know how supper was going. She slipped her phone out of her pocket, ignoring Papa's glare. The color drained from her face and she shoved the phone under her thigh.

"Are you okay?" Of course Mama had noticed.

"Fine. Supper is really good. Thank you."

"There's brownies for dessert." Mama dished them up without waiting for a response.

Dani knew she'd have to look at her phone again eventually, but the rain had eased by the time she pulled back into the drive of her new home and she still wanted a peek at the old barn. *But first, whiskey.* Inside, Dani dug in the cupboards for the cups. Mama definitely had not put them where Dani would have. On the third try, she found the cups. Bypassing the small juice cups with floral prints, she chose a large plastic cup with some football player she didn't recognize on the side. She filled it with whiskey and headed back out. Heavy clouds still blanketed the sky, but it was barely sprinkling as Dani made the short walk across the backyard to the falling down barn.

She paused just inside the barn door and sipped the whiskey, swirling it around her mouth. It stung. Definitely lighter fluid quality, but it would do the trick. At first glance, the barn was empty. No cool old implements or large antiques to excite the junkers on those TV shows. But around the edges were small signs of the life that once was. A pair of rusted old sheep shears hung on the wall by the loop in the handle. A wooden cane hung nearby - a shepherd's crook, she figured. Over the workbench at the back hung an old hammer, a square, and some kind of chisel. None of it was worth money, but it told Dani more about the house's previous owner. Clearly a hardworking sheep farmer, but also a woodworker, at least in his spare time. If he built the workbench, he was a good one. The workbench wasn't fancy, but it was clean, efficient, and the only thing on the whole place that was old and not falling apart. She kicked through piles of dirt over to the workbench and ran her fingers along the top. Dings and scars spoke of difficult projects completed here. Numbers written to the side in pencil showed planning. The handwriting reminded her of Papa's, and her own. The 5 formed with two strokes instead of one, the occasional loops blended with what Mama called "chicken scratch." But the writing was bigger than Papa's and neater than her own. She wondered who had lived here, if maybe a relative had, at some point, worked in this very barn. She knew it belonged in the family, but it had only ever been rented to farm hands or city folks on a short adventure. Maybe Grandpa had worked in here, though it felt odd to her, if someone else was living in the house. But Papa said Grandma had always treated the renters like family, so maybe. She took a swig of her whiskey, letting it burn straight down her throat this time. She kept her head back, examining the roof. Cobwebs and straw, no doubt left over from a bird's nest, hung down from the rafters. The sky peeked through gaps in the tin roof. The dark was lowering fast, helped by the storm clouds.

Another swig of whiskey and Dani wandered to the next wall of the barn. She walked along a thick wooden rail, or maybe an old post, one arm out for balance. Junk was piled in the foot or so between the rail and the wall. Probably all trash. There was rusted metal in the pile, though. She nudged it with her toe. It didn't move, so it was big or heavy or both. Another swig of whiskey. The cup was almost empty and Dani was feeling brave, or the whiskey-induced equivalent thereof. She pulled out her phone.

"I'll find you."

It was still there. *Well of course it's still there. Where the hell would it go?* She took a screenshot and sent it to Kat.

"No, he won't. I don't even know exactly where you are."

"You do, too. Find My Friends. But what about my car? If he goes looking maybe he'll see it."

"IF he looks MAYBE he'll see it. Deep breath. And trade the car in if you're worried about it."

"Not sure I make enough for that. You think he'll look?"

"No. He's too lazy for that and you know it." Dani finished her whiskey and sat on the rail, looking out the barn door. If it was in better shape, she could park in here. But the last thing she needed was a rickety old barn collapsing on her little car.

Larger drops of rain began to patter down, making a kind of music on the barn's tin roof. Dani took a deep breath. Maybe it wasn't exactly where she wanted to be, but in this moment, this place was heaven. Thunder cracked and Dani rose to look out the door at the clouds. A darker band was headed her way. She'd get wet either way, but since she hadn't left the back light on, Dani thought she'd better make a break for the house while she could still see the door.

The rain was cold, but Dani felt a childlike delight as she splashed through the grass to the back door. Inside, she leaned back against the door, smiling. She looked down at the water dripping to the floor. *Well, there are perks to living alone.* Dani stripped off her jeans, soaked at the bottom, and pulled her t-shirt over her head. She dropped both on top of the washer and said a silent prayer that the ancient thing still worked. That was a problem for later. Right now, she wanted whiskey. She stepped into the kitchen and felt a wet wind against her arm. *Crap. The windows.* Dani set her cup on the counter and set about finding and closing the open windows. Only the dining room window needed mopping up, thankfully. Crisis averted, Dani poured herself another glass of whiskey and flopped onto the couch. It wasn't the softest in the world, but it would do. A remote lay on the arm of the couch. Odds were slim, but it was worth a shot. She turned the TV on. Static. She flipped through a few more channels of static before giving up and turning the TV off. No TV. No Internet yet. Dani swigged her whiskey and considered her options. On such a rainy night, reading in bed was sounding best. Dani pushed herself up off the couch. She retrieved her phone from the pocket of her jeans and headed to the stairs, turning off lights on her way. Thunder rumbled and Dani stood at the foot of the stairs, sipping her whiskey. The sights and sounds from upstairs had mostly faded from memory, but she still felt uneasy about heading up with only the stair light on. Books and bed were a strong pull, though, especially with a large amount of whiskey in her system. She climbed the stairs slowly and turned toward her bedroom. All was dark, just the stairway light behind her. It was creepy like this. Dani moved quickly to the room and flipped on the light. She set her phone on the bed and her whiskey on the floor. She snagged her toothbrush and toothpaste and darted to the bathroom. She felt like a little kid running from monsters in the dark. Teeth brushed, she forced herself to turn off the bathroom light and walk slowly to the stair light switch. She flicked the light off and ran the few feet to her bedroom where she slammed the door closed against the dark. She dropped to her bed, laughing. *Freedom might be kind of fun after all.*

~ 2 ~

The incessant dinging of a phone alarm roused Dani, who was immediately aware of a suffocating heat. She rolled over to turn the phone alarm off and every muscle in her body, it seemed, screamed in protest. She nearly dropped her phone as it came in contact with her blistered palms. Dani groaned. Morning chores were going to hurt. She got up gingerly, pulled on jeans, decided the calves and pigs wouldn't care if she wore a bra, and pulled a shirt on. She wandered blearily down the stairs and realized her mother had forgotten one very important thing: coffee. Dani considered dropping to the floor and throwing a good old fashioned tantrum, but figured her body was sore enough. She settled for texting Kat instead.

"No coffee?!?! What is this place? Are you being held against your will? Text me avocado if you are." Dani smiled. No one knew how to verbally tantrum quite like Kat.

"No avocados here, either."

"That's it! I'm sending a rescue team."

Dani pulled on her boots. Papa would have coffee. She just had to get through chores first. The calves were fine. All there, all hungry, and one even licked her as she checked their water. The boars grunted at her until their feed pans were filled, but they weren't threatening, just gruff. As she pulled open the door at her final stop, the finishing barn, Dani caught sight of the thin white gilt pushing through a gate next to the feeder. She groaned and decided to leave her out. She could clearly get back in if she wanted.

Back in the house, Dani threw on a sports bra whose seams protested but held and grabbed her keys. She kicked out of her muck boots and into her flip flops. Hopefully Papa wouldn't need help with anything. Coffee was calling.

Papa was hunched over a bowl of bran flakes when Dani pushed open the front door.

"Chores done?" She nodded and pulled a mug from the cabinet, trying to ignore her aching arms. "Gilt out again?" Dani nodded again. She poured her coffee and dropped into a chair across from Papa. "Catch that snake in the dairy barn?" She looked up from her coffee to find Papa grinning. "Ah, so you are awake." He chuckled and Dani couldn't help but join him.

"No snakes, Papa, but I was looking at that old work bench in the barn last night. Anybody from our family ever use it?"

"No. Dad said it was included in rent." Was it her imagination, or was Papa a little short with her?

"Just wondered. Looks like it's seen some use." She glanced at the clock. "I better get back down there. They're installing my Internet today so I can get my classes set up."

"What all are you teaching this year?" Dani smiled as they lapsed into an easy discussion of books and authors, needed writing skills, and his opinions on her chosen reading. Papa was a voracious reader, and he loved to hear her stories from class. Mostly, though, she knew he was just proud of her accomplishments and wanted to hear about them.

Three coffees and an apple later, full and feeling better about life, Dani was headed back to the house to meet the Internet installer. With classes starting soon, she was anxious to get to work. Teaching online wouldn't be the same as seeing her students in person, but it would be safer and she'd be able to make her own schedule. She didn't like people and driving in the city anyway, right? Right.

"You got this, Jo. I am talking to myself. Wow." Dani shook her head as she pulled into the drive to find the KNet truck already waiting in the drive. Breakfast with Papa had taken longer than she'd realized. She parked and got out, phone at the ready. A tall, thin man unfolded himself from the truck and Dani felt herself stop breathing and take a step back toward her car. She unlocked her phone.

"Hi! I'm Finn. You ordered Internet? Are you okay?" *Finn. His name is Finn. He has red hair. He's wearing glasses. Finn. It's not him.* Dani coached herself and slowly, she felt her breath return and her heart rate slow. She strained to smile.

"Yes. I did. Just let me know what you need."

"A signature here first." Finn stretched the clipboard out to her, obviously taking care not to step closer. Her fear must have been painfully obvious. She felt herself blush and hoped he would think it was just the heat. "Alright, now I just need to grab your equipment and see where we can get the best signal." Dani nodded and stepped up to the back door, waiting for him. He dropped a router into a satchel at his side and strode toward her. "Since you're doing WiFi, the exact location is flexible, but I'm guessing upstairs would be best. You just tell me anywhere you want to try or anywhere that's off-limits." Dani took a deep breath. Yup, he had clearly noticed she was uncomfortable.

"Upstairs is fine. Wherever you need." She led the way to the stairs. When they reached the top, she pointed to the left. "There's a big empty room that way with several windows. Plaster is falling, but it's safe." She pointed to the right. "Two rooms down that way. Fewer windows, but again, you can use them if you want." She stepped to the side. Finn seemed to think for a moment.

"Left is West, right?" Dani nodded. "Okay, then that's our best bet." Dani nodded again and led the way down the hall. As she touched the doorknob, she felt the temperature drop. *Odd. No windows should be open in here.* She pushed open the door and froze in place. A woman faced her, wearing a square-necked white dress with cap sleeves and an A-line skirt. She stood in front of an open window, and a light breeze fluttered her skirt. She met Dani's gaze, then turned around and stepped out the window.

"No!" Dani slammed the door wide open and ran to the window. She stopped short. It was closed. Plaster crashed down behind her. Dani spun around to find Finn standing at the door. He looked uncertain if he should enter or run away.

"Dani, right? Are you okay?" Dani stood, mouth open, but managed to nod.

"I. I'm sorry. I thought I saw . . . something."

Finn forced a laugh. "Haunted house?"

"I'm not sure. Maybe." Finn's smile disappeared.

"Oh. Well, let's get your Internet set up so you can document it. Maybe you'll get famous. Or maybe one of those ghost hunter guys will come get rid of it for you." He was clearly trying to joke, but Dani was pretty sure it didn't raise either of their spirits. She pulled open the window she'd seen the woman step through. A breeze would feel good while Finn worked, she told herself, but she snuck a glance at the ground, just to be sure.

"Do you need anything to drink? I'm going to go grab some water myself."

"No, thanks, this will only take a minute. If you want to grab your computer or phone, we can make sure we get you logged on before I leave." Finn turned to work and Dani raced down the stairs. She did need a drink, but she opted for whiskey inside a travel coffee mug so that Finn wouldn't know. He'd be busy for a bit, so she stepped out onto the front porch, enjoying the breeze and sipping her whiskey. She sent a quick message to Kat to see if she wanted to video call after her Internet was up and running. She needed to tell someone about the woman. Someone who wouldn't immediately institutionalize her for it.

Dani stepped carefully down off the front porch. This part of the yard needed some work, she noted, but it could be very cute. Some flowers in front, maybe add some steps at the side. She walked around to the west side of the house, studying the ground. The woman wasn't real. She knew that. And yet . . . it had felt, looked so real. She looked up. There was the open window. She followed a straight line down the side of the house to an overgrown flower bed. She would look closer later. Maybe while she chatted with Kat. She looked up at the open window again and caught a flutter of white. Just her imagination. She shook her head and took a deep swig of whiskey before heading back in and up the stairs to check on Finn.

"Okay, you are all set." Finn handed over a sheet with her temporary password that he'd encouraged her to change. She wouldn't. "You know, this room feels great. You should really fix it up and sleep in here. I don't know how else you survive without air conditioning."

"I've thought about it, but this room is pretty rough. Thanks for helping me get connected, though." He waited while she connected to the new network with her phone. Sure all was working properly, Finn got another signature and slung his bag over his shoulder. Dani followed Finn down the stairs and to his truck. He waved before pulling out of the drive and she ducked her head. She wandered into the old barn, tracing the grooves in the old workbench as she checked the Internet signal on her phone. Not bad, even out here. Kat had said yes to a call, so Dani started a video chat.

"Hey! So show me the place. Where are you now? Tell me this isn't your bedroom."

"Dude. Slow down. Do you think I live in *Little House on the Prairie*? This is the old barn. It's weird. It was mostly cleared out, but these few things are still here. I don't get why they didn't take these." Dani showed her the shepherd's crook, clippers, and work bench surface.

"Creepy. Somebody didn't want to remember that, I guess. Or maybe he was just done farming and building? But I want to see this house. Is it cute? Are we fixing it up? Are we staying there awhile or do we want out?"

Ignoring the flurry of questions, Dani stepped out of the barn and showed Kat the house. As she walked around the east side to show her the front porch, she told Kat about the woman.

"You saw a Woman in White? You have to find out what happened there."

"What's a Woman in White?"

"A woman wearing white. Obviously. She's a ghost. Some kind of tragedy happened there. She could have been murdered, maybe her kids died, maybe her husband cheated, but something traumatic for sure."

"Well, she just stepped out the window."

"Oh, so maybe she died by suicide after whatever happened."

"Lovely. Just what the mentally unstable divorcee needs. A suicidal ghost roommate." Dani turned to the west side of the house. "This is the window," Dani stopped. The woman stood in the window. "Do you see that?"

"See what? That's the window she stepped out of?"

"She's there now. Do you seriously not see her?" Dani glanced down at the phone screen. Nothing. Her eyes snapped back to the window. The woman was there. She heard a scream as the woman stepped out and plummeted to the ground just feet in front of her and disappeared.

"Dani, are you okay? Dani? Why did you scream? What happened?"

"You didn't see that? She just did it again. She hit the ground right there." Dani pointed the camera at the tangle of weeds and wildflowers. "Right here." She stepped into the weeds and thrust her hand into the mess. Pawing through the weeds and flowers, Dani felt her anxiety rise.

"What are you doing? Dani, she's not there. I didn't see anything."

"I'm seeing her for a reason. I have to find something."

"What?"

"I don't know." Dani's fingers scraped something hard. "Hang on." She dropped her phone in the yard and returned to yanking stems aside with both hands. Her fingers scraped against a rock. She yanked weeds from the ground, bringing it into view. It was jet black and smooth. "There's a rock," she shouted to Kat, who she hoped was still on the phone.

"Of course there's a rock. You live on a farm again. Dani, come on." Kat sounded worried, but this was real. Dani knew it. It had to be. Finally, she had the entire rock exposed. She grabbed the phone again and showed Kat.

"Look. I am not crazy." Dani swiped a hand across the top of the rock, removing a layer of dirt and dead weeds. She felt a texture in one corner and scrubbed harder. "Hey, it says something here." She knelt on the oblong rock, about two feet wide at its widest point. "1973 JML. What on earth does that mean?" No response. "Kat?"

"I'm here. Dani, something is weird here. You have to find out what's going on. But you have to be safe."

"What do you mean?" Dani knew, though, and she felt sick.

"If your Woman in White died by suicide," she trailed off. "You can't go down that road again."

Dani was quiet for a moment, tracing her fingers over the year and the letters. "Initials, maybe?"

"Maybe. But Dani, did you hear me?"

"I know. I won't. I got my fresh start. No more scars." She glanced down at her forearm, forever a reminder of her lowest low. "I'm seeing her for a reason, though, don't you think?"

"I do. I think you have to find out what happened to her. I don't know why, but I know you have to."

Dani nodded. "I'm on it." She sat back on her heels and picked up her forgotten whiskey. She took a swig as Kat rattled on about research sources for her Woman in White, as if she hadn't also done research in her day. "Hey, can we talk about something else? How's the pilot?"

"The pilot? Oh, you mean the hang glider? He's fine, I guess. I dumped him a couple days ago. I'm keeping the rodeo guy for a little bit, though." Dani laughed and relaxed into the normalcy that Kat's dating exploits brought. As she half-listened to details about another guy whose name she wouldn't bother to learn, Dani went back into the house and topped off her whiskey. She made a quick sandwich and settled on the couch to eat. Kat had moved on to the classes they would each be teaching this semester. "I got stuck with a Comp I, but the others should be okay. A couple Comp IIs and Intro to Lit. What about you?"

"Three sections of Comp II and one Intro to Lit. It'll be weird online, but at least I didn't get Comp I."

"Ugh. Lucky." They commiserated about freshmen for a little bit.

"I should probably go make sure I can get my computer logged on and start getting ready for classes. I feel like I'm behind already." Dani stretched her aching muscles out along the couch and brushed some stray sandwich crumbs off of her chest.

"You're not. You've totally got this. You're teaching the same stuff, you just have to change your methods a little to work online."

"I know. And I can use videos if I get them made, but still. It's just so different. Everything is so different." The two sat in silence, both thinking over the past year. The hell they'd been through. "Thank you for pulling me out."

"Thank you for getting out. Love you."

"Love you, too." Dani hung up, leaned back into the couch, and cried.

~ 3 ~

That night, Dani decided to do chores early. She'd gotten the basic framework for her Comp II classes set up and she needed a brain break. Besides, maybe Mama would answer questions about the rock she'd found if she got there early enough to help make supper. She brushed her teeth and chugged a glass of water before heading out to subject her aching arms and hands to chores again.

Carrying water to the boars was the worst. She felt the skin of one of her blisters slip and knew it would be oozing and sore. Still, she gritted her teeth and pushed ahead. Soon, her palms would be calloused and she'd be a stronger, better version of herself. That or it would kill her. Either way, these blisters wouldn't last forever.

At the finishing barn, Dani sighed at the skinny white gilt, out again. Or still. "Look, if you're going to be a pain in my ass, you need a name. You're too skinny to be Bacon." Dani propped open the gate to the gilt's pen and chased her back inside. "Ham would require you to put on a few pounds, too. How about . . . Anika? Worst boss ever. You remind me of her." Dani slid the rod in to hold the pen shut and checked the feeders. All good. "Good night, Anika. Stay put, would you?" Dani imagined she heard Anika snort derisively and laughed as she left.

Chores completed, Dani made her way back toward the house. She pulled her phone from her pocket and turned on some music as she reached WiFi range. Sometimes, it was just too quiet around here. She crossed the driveway and was nearly on the sidewalk to the back door when she heard a thump from the barn. She pivoted and cautiously approached the barn door. Probably just an animal looking for shelter, but still, her heart raced and irrational images of him hiding in the barn flashed through her mind. She paused outside the door to turn on her phone's flashlight. She edged slowly around the corner. Nothing. Flashing her light to the corners, Dani saw that no human or animal was lurking in the barn. *Something had to make that noise, though.* She stepped inside, eyes still flitting about for any sign of danger. Then, an awful thought occurred to her. She hadn't checked the rafters. Dani dropped to a crouch and surveyed the rafters. Nothing. She let out a breath and stood, stepping toward the work bench. Her fingers traced the numbers written on its dented surface. How could this handwriting be so similar to her own?

In the next instant, a flutter in the rafters caused Dani to drop to the ground, scooting on her bottom beneath the protection of the work bench as her heart rate skyrocketed. She peered out from under the workbench. A crow, or maybe a raven? She'd have to look up the difference later. Feeling ridiculous, she leaned back against the wall of the barn and took a deep breath. She really was on edge for a bird, even an ominous looking black one, to send her scurrying for cover. Opening her eyes, an odd shadow on the bottom of the workbench caught her eye. She reached out tentatively toward it, probing with her fingertips. Cold metal. She leaned forward. A gun? Surely not. Why would a gun be under an old workbench not used in her lifetime?

Dani pulled her phone from her pocket, its flashlight still on. Yes, that was most definitely a gun. A leather holster had been screwed to the bottom of the wooden workbench and the gun was tucked snugly inside. Why, though? Guns were not uncommon out here, but mostly they were rifles meant for dealing with coyotes and were kept in the house. Why would someone have a handgun carefully hidden in the barn? Dani pulled the gun from its holster. She turned it over in her hands, trying to figure out how to eject the clip she knew was in the grip. It looked so easy in the movies. Eventually, she found a button on the side and the clip slid out onto the ground. *Probably not good.* She retrieved the clip and noted that it was full. *Whoever left the pistol here was serious about protection. But from what? How do I check the chamber on this thing? No sense in accidentally shooting something.* She remembered her favorite TV show character firing a pistol. He'd pulled the slide back. She pulled back. The slide moved smoothly. Whoever's gun this was, they'd taken care of it. A coppery colored bullet glinted in the chamber. Dani tipped it into her palm. *Who was this intended for?*

Inside, Dani made a sandwich from the sparse supplies in the fridge. After the run-in with the bird, she couldn't face a family meal. Enough was enough. She would need to make a grocery run soon if she didn't want to eat sandwiches or keep going to her parents' for every meal. *And coffee. Definitely need coffee.* She ate standing in the kitchen, examining the pistol she'd set on the counter when she'd realized how hungry she was. Maybe Kat would have ideas. She snapped a picture and sent it to her. The response was immediate.

"Why do you have a gun? Is that Dean's gun? Where did you get that? He's not coming to get you, I promise. He does NOT know where you are." Dani smiled. *Oh, Kat.*

"I found it in the barn, under the workbench. It might be the same one he uses in *Supernatural*...not sure. I don't know much about pistols." She decided to ignore the last part of Kat's text. He might find her. She wasn't that far from her parents' house and he did know where that was, after all.

"Who hides a gun under a workbench?"

"Great question. Doesn't seem like a place you'd need a gun."

"Maybe it has something to do with the woman you keep seeing."

"It has to, right? Or it's one hell of a coincidence." Dani shoved the last bit of sandwich into her mouth and set her phone down. She picked up the gun, holding it in her right hand, finger on the trigger guard. It wasn't overly heavy, but the barrel was long enough to be awkward. Granted, it wasn't loaded. Maybe he would never find her, but Dani decided having this pistol handy would make her feel safer. Just in case. She shifted the pistol to her left hand, reaching for the clip when she noticed something etched into the grip. It looked professionally done, but it didn't appear to be a manufacturer's marking. It was just three letters. JML. *The rock. The woman. But surely a woman in the 1960s or 1970s wouldn't have had a customized gun, would she?* Etched into the right side, so either the shooter was left-handed or the customization was meant to sit in the shooter's palm. Not that it mattered, but Dani found herself wondering which was true. She set the gun back down. Almost without thinking, she poured herself a tall whiskey. Papa had seemed close-mouthed about the workbench, but maybe the rock would be a way in. She texted her mother. "Found a rock in the flowerbed with 1973 JML etched into it. What's that about?" When her answer didn't come immediately, Dani sent a picture of the pistol grip to Kat.

"Well that answers that question. Definitely connected to your woman in white."

"But how? You think those are her initials? Seems weird she'd have them on a gun."

"Maybe she was a badass. But probably a man's, you're right."

Dani slammed the clip into the pistol, but didn't cock it. No sense in creating extra danger when she was so unfamiliar with the gun. She shoved her phone in her pocket, grabbed her whiskey, and headed to her bedroom. *Maybe I'm a badass. Gun in one hand, whiskey in the other. Like some bad western hero.* She smiled at the thought. As she reached the top of the stairs and the halfway point of her whiskey, a flicker of light to her left caught her eye. *What the hell? No one was up here, and that door had been closed, right?* She set her whiskey down on the top step and gripped the pistol in both hands. Pivoting to the left, she crept down the hall toward the big room at the end of the hall. Another flicker of light. Bigger than a firefly, but just as fast. *Was that a breeze?* Dani pressed her back against the wall to her left, stretching her neck to look into the bedroom. *Nothing.* Her gun following her eyes, Dani shifted to the other wall and craned to see into the room. *Still nothing.* She'd have to actually go in. Calling up all of her TV crime show watching experience, Dani stepped into the room and scanned it, left to right, gun continuing to follow her eyes. The window above the stone was open again, but nothing else seemed off. She was grateful that the house was old enough not to have closets. One less spot for him to hide.

Dani relaxed, dropping the gun to her side and realizing that she hadn't pulled back the slide to load a bullet into the chamber anyway. *Fat lot of good that would have done.* She crossed to the window and looked out. Why was the woman so bent on having this open? If the apparition from earlier was any indication, she'd jumped out of the window at some point, so why would she want to relive that? Dani retrieved her whiskey and returned to sit in the center of the bedroom, clearing some fallen plaster from the floor. She looked around at the room, trying to imagine it before it had been abandoned. Wide wooden trim flanked the floors, doors, and windows. It had most recently been painted white, but it was flaking off to reveal an olive green color underneath. Maybe at one point it had been a simple, beautiful wood grain. The house was certainly old enough. A late 1800s build, if she remembered the family story correctly. Either way, it wouldn't take much to knock the crumbling plaster down and replace it with sheetrock, put a fresh coat of white paint on the trim, maybe a slate blue color on the walls. She looked down at the floor, brushing plaster dust aside. Hardwood. Definitely worth refinishing. Dani drained her whiskey and stood to go get more. Suddenly, a strong breeze blew in the open window and Dani felt dizzy. Her vision softened, as if white tulle had been pulled over her eyes.

The bedroom was complete now, with olive green trim, beige walls, and a bed against the far wall. The window was still open, with the breeze pushing against heavy drapes patterned with gold and green. The bed was neatly made with crisp, hospital corners. It looked like something out of a 70s magazine. On the side of the bed closest to the open window was a night stand. A simple lamp and a book with a tasseled bookmark were on top. On the lower shelf stood a water glass and a stack of magazines. On the other side of the bed, the nightstand was empty but for the lamp. No sign of life, or at least not of personality. Did someone sleep on that side, or was it empty? Was she judging someone's bedside table choices or was she witnessing the loneliness of her Woman in White?

As quickly as it came, the dizziness and gauzy vision left. The room was once again dark, dirty, and in desperate need of renovation. The only thing that remained was the breeze through the open window. Dani shook her head. She caught a glimpse of the woman's hair as she dropped out of view outside the window. This time, she felt no need to rush to the window to check for her body. She wasn't there, Dani knew, but she had just been here, Ms. JML, and she'd shown Dani something. *But why? Why just a scene of her bedroom? Couldn't she have just shown me whatever happened and been done with it?*

"Come on, man! What do you want with me?" Dani turned and left the room, heading down the stairs to grab her whiskey bottle. *Might as well have it easily accessible.* As she started back up the stairs, her phone buzzed. Dani glanced at her phone. A text from her mother letting her know that she could ride to church with them if she wanted, but no answer to her question about the stone. In other words, she was expected to attend church, whether in her own car or theirs. Dani groaned. She'd love to skip Sunday School, but he knew the church and might cruise by looking for her car, so she'd better take her mother up on the ride.

"I'll be up to your place by 8!" She added the exclamation mark in hopes that her mother would read it as excitement instead of the very real dread she was feeling. No sense in mentioning the stone again. If Mama didn't want to tell her by text, she wasn't going to. Maybe later, in person, but Dani wasn't holding her breath.

~ 4 ~

"It is well. It is well with my soul." Dani sang automatically. *It is not at all well with my soul*, she thought. The morning had been every bit as awful as she imagined. Little old ladies she vaguely remembered asking where her husband was. Either Mama forgot to tell them or they forgot she did. Her mother's friends hugging her just a little too long and asking just a little too brightly how she was doing being back home. She couldn't bring herself to tell the little old ladies that she was divorced. They seemed to remember her so fondly and she couldn't bear to break their hearts and shatter their image of her as the sweet girl who sang off-key in the church choir. As for her mother's friends, well, what could she do but endure the hugs and tell them it was nice to be home?

During the sermon, Dani doodled on the bulletin, filling in the spaces in the letters. Pastor read the story of Jesus walking out to his disciples in the boat. Dani noted that he skipped the part where the disciples thought Jesus was a ghost. *Probably not relevant to his point*, she told herself. *That or Christians aren't supposed to believe in ghosts. Wonder what the little old ladies would make of me if they knew I was divorced and seeing a ghost on the regular. Do they still burn people at the stake?* Dani smirked at her private joke. She'd have to remember to text that to Kat later, when her mother wasn't sitting close enough to smack her on the back of the head if she dared get out her phone. Instead, she found some white space on the bulletin and began a list of things she needed to get done. Top of the list was course prep. She had yet to cobble together a syllabus for any of her classes, mostly because she had yet to select any readings, and the spiral just continued from there. She vowed to get through at least one syllabus today. As she laid out the steps she'd need to take to be ready to teach, Dani kept seeing the 70s bedroom. She added "Knock down bedroom plaster" to her list. She'd need to rehab the house at some point, anyway. Or someone would. Might as well be her.

After church, with no getaway car, Dani was forced to wait while her parents talked to every single member of the congregation, or close enough to it that her stomach started trying to eat itself out of a combination of anxiety and hunger. She leaned against the wall just a couple feet behind them, watching as person after person approached. They didn't even have to seek people out. *This must be what celebrity is like.* Dani glanced again at her to-do list, trying to work out a rough schedule for the day in her head. *The syllabus really has to come first. Otherwise, I'll just keep putting it off.*

"Hi, Dani?" Dani jerked her head up to see a young woman about her age standing in front of her. "I don't want to interrupt, but I heard you're living in the house south of your parents'. My family was the last to live there, I think." Dani still leaned silently against the wall, uncertain what this girl could want and still a bit in shock that someone was talking to her. Just to her. "I think it's nice that someone's living there again. I hope you'll fix it up. Whatever you've heard, it's not true. At least not all of it. I loved growing up in that house. It's a good home, or it can be again. I'm sure it's in awful shape now." Dani nodded. This girl didn't seem to be able to stop talking. *When was the last time she took a breath?* "Sorry, I don't usually just talk to people like this. I just. I wanted you to know. That I think it's good, I mean." Finally, she stopped talking. It took Dani a moment to realize that she was really done.

"Oh. Thank you, I think. What do you mean, though, about what I might have heard about the house?" The girl might be a little off, but maybe she could help with the mystery ghost.

"No one told you? It's haunted." That last bit she practically whispered. "I mean, people say it is. It's not, obviously. Ghosts and all aren't real. Everyone knows that." *Did they?* The girl didn't even look like she believed what she was saying now. "But ever since we left that house, people have been saying it."

"Would you like to come see it?" *What am I doing? I don't want to hang out with her. But she knows things.* "We could trade names and numbers."

"Oh my gosh. I got so caught up I didn't even introduce myself. I'm Marie Levee. I would love to come see the place again. I always did love living out there in the country. I'm back in town now, of course." Dani thought she'd never get Marie refocused on trading contact information so they could set up a time to meet. It would be hard to keep her on track long enough to learn more about her ghost. On the other hand, Marie seemed unlikely to notice if Dani questioned her more intensely than she should. It seemed a fair trade.

Lunch was quiet and Dani thought she'd escape the whole Sunday morning ritual unscathed. She only had a few bites of lunch left, after which she could excuse herself to go work on her class prep. Papa cleared his throat. *Oh, no. Here it comes.*

"I saw you met Marie." The comment seemed innocent enough, but Dani sensed danger.

"Something like that. Does she ever stop talking?" *Stay neutral as long as possible.* Dani was sure Marie knew something, and she was equally sure that Papa knew it, too.

"Not usually. What'd she have to say?" There it was. Papa was fishing, trying to determine how much damage control he needed to do to cover whatever past he was hiding.

"Something about ghosts not being real and her family living down in the old hand's house. I kind of lost track." *That's at least partially true. Do you go to hell for partially true?* "She wants to come see her old house, so she may come by sometime. We didn't set a date."

"Ghosts?" Papa shook his head. "No such thing. Marie's a little off. I'm sure you could tell." *What is it about ghosts that has Papa spooked?*

"I caught that. Still, no harm in her seeing her old bedroom or whatever. She thought they were the last people to live here, so it's probably still the same paint and carpet and all." Papa nodded and shoved a fork full of green beans into his mouth. He didn't look up from his plate as he chewed.

Either the conversation was over or Papa was choosing his next words very carefully. Dani watched him swallow his beans before settling back in his chair.

"That was delicious, Mama." Dani waited. Papa examined his dessert choices and popped open the plastic container holding a frosted chocolate cake.

"Just keep your head on straight." There it was, the admonishment Dani had been waiting for. This one was mild, especially given that she was pretty sure Papa was hiding something Marie could expose.

"I'm just letting her see the house, Papa, not starting a cult." Dani took a piece of chocolate cake and shoved a bite in her mouth. She didn't really like cake, but it gave her something to focus on besides her father's disapproving look. She swallowed. "Oh, can I borrow a hammer?"

~ 5 ~

One syllabus down. One to go. Thank God I can use the same one for all the Comp classes. Dani flipped her computer shut and stretched her arms toward the ceiling. She'd sat still for far too long. She shoved the computer back into her bag, noting the drops of sweat that had collected underneath it on her thighs. *This place needs air conditioning.* She stood and carried her glass to the kitchen. She filled it with tap water first, chugging it quickly. The barn was in her line of sight out the kitchen sink window. Dani wondered if the raven was still in the rafters. She'd looked up the difference. Crows were apparently small, about the size of pigeons, and her black bird had been much larger. There were other differences, but she'd been a little too scared to notice the shagginess of his feathers or shape of his tail. Apparently, ravens tended to travel in pairs, too. If there was a second raven in the barn, it had chosen not to be a dick and scare her. She wondered if they had a nest in the barn or nearby. Was it even nesting season? A thunk sounded from upstairs, and Dani felt her heartbeat quicken as her eyes instinctively snapped toward the ceiling. JML or falling plaster. Maybe both. Either way, it was time to get to work. Dani rinsed out the travel coffee mug and refilled it with whiskey. She grabbed the hammer from the counter and headed up the stairs.

In the big bedroom, Dani sipped her whiskey and considered where to start. *Should have asked Papa for a ladder, too.* "Alright, J, this is going to look like I'm breaking your room, but I have to before I can fix it. We'll negotiate colors later. I'm not such a huge fan of that olive green you had on the trim." A piece of plaster crashed from the ceiling to her right. Dani jumped, then cocked her hip. "I said we'll talk about it later." She took a drink of her whiskey and set it on the floor near the door. She walked toward a crack in the plaster on the opposite side of the room, on the same wall as J's window, but at the other end. "Here we go, J. Let's see if we can get this place cleaned up." Dani swung the hammer at the crack. The plaster cracked and fell, a thick cloud of dust rising from it. Dani coughed. She'd need a mask. Dani retreated to her room and rummaged through her clothes. *Should probably put some in the dresser.* "Aha!" Dani held up a bedazzled black bandanna, a leftover from an incredibly boozy girls' night out. She unfolded it and tied it around her neck, pulling it up and over her mouth and nose. *Perfect.*

An hour later, coated in sweat, Dani stopped to check her progress and grab a drink. She'd cleared most of J's wall. That was how she thought of it now. Some plaster remained around the windows. She'd need to pry the trim boards out before finishing that part. And she wasn't tall enough to get all the way to the ceiling. Still, it was progress. "What do ya think, J? We'll put sheetrock up and paint and it'll be good as new." No plaster fell from the ceiling, so Dani decided J must be okay with it. She glanced at her phone. She had time to make a bit more progress before chores. Between this job and chores, her hands were all blisters and bruises, but somehow she felt better than she had in a long time. One more swig of whiskey. *I should probably get some water before chores.* She swung the hammer, settling into a rhythm and watching the old crumble away.

After chores and chasing the damn white gilt back into her pen again, Dani went inside and washed her hands before surveying her supper options. *Nothing appetizing. Of course. Mom's it is.* She sniffed her armpit and made a face. *Gross. No way a quick sponge bath will fix this.* Dani groaned aloud, but trudged toward the bathroom to rinse off in a quick shower before heading to her parents' for supper. *I have got to get my own groceries. But I do need a pry bar and ladder anyway, so I guess tonight is inevitable. Tomorrow, though, I go to the store.*

Dried off and dressed, Dani leaned in the doorway of J's bedroom, surveying the damage. The entire room was coated in a layer of white dust. *A fitting residence for a ghost if ever there was one.* The breeze blew in through J's window and kept the dust from getting too thick in that area of the room, almost as if the White Woman was keeping her favorite spot clean.

"Okay, J, I'm headed up for supper. I'll be back and maybe we'll pry off some of that trim tonight." A firefly flashed through the window and Dani nodded, taking it as a sign of agreement.

Downstairs, Dani swished water through her mouth to reduce the whiskey smell, grabbed her keys, and slipped on her flip-flops. Her little blue car was waiting in its spot, but Dani walked past it. She stepped slowly into the barn, eyes trained on the rafters. She spotted the raven when his shiny black eye caught the light. His feathers did look a little rougher than other birds, almost shaggy. *Definitely a raven, then. No nest, though. Do ravens even build nests? And no mate that I see. Are you alone, little guy?* Dani stared at the raven, who stared right back, head cocked, one black bead of an eye trained on her. He hopped sideways on the beam, edging closer to her. He stilled and stared again. Suddenly, he ducked his head and swooped down from the rafter to the workbench, just inches from Dani's face. She let out a startled cry. The raven was unperturbed. Back to her, he strutted across the workbench, then cocked his head back to look at her. Dani felt oddly as if he was asking her to come with him. She took a slow step toward the workbench. He watched. She took another. He turned away and walked to the edge of the bench, back still to her. He pivoted to face her. Dani continued toward him, slowly. *He's waiting for me. That's ridiculous. Birds don't wait for people.* Still, Dani walked to the raven. Finally, she stood at the bench and waited. The raven held her gaze for a moment, then turned and pecked at the underside of the shelf positioned above the workbench. It had once held all manner of tools, Dani was certain, but it was empty now. The raven turned back toward her, a fleck of white in its beak. He strutted toward her and Dani instinctively backed up a step. He dropped the white onto the bench and Dani almost thought he looked annoyed with her. He backed up. She stepped forward in what she thought must be the most awkward dance ever. Paper. *Probably picking a label off the bench,* Dani though, but then, it looked homemade. Not the kind of thing that would have a label.

"What is this?" The raven caught her eye again, stared for a moment, and swooped back up to his perch in the rafters. Dani leaned down to look under the shelf. An envelope was stuck under the edge of the mounting bracket. She stood and looked at the raven. She could swear he nodded. Dani nodded back, then stooped to retrieve the envelope. She turned it over. No writing. Her phone buzzed and Dani jumped. "Oh, good Lord." She pulled it from her pocket. Her mother, wanting to know if she was coming for supper. She replied and walked toward the barn door, turning back before she left to look at the raven one more time. "Thank you." She had no idea what she was thanking him for, but it seemed right.

Between bites of garden fresh cucumbers and pork chops, Dani told her parents of her progress in the big upstairs bedroom. She left out the parts about talking to JML. They wouldn't have believed her anyway. Her papa agreed to loan her a pry bar and ladder, and her mother even offered to come help her do the work the next night. *So far, so good.*

"I'll definitely let you know if I get to it tomorrow, mama. Hey, did you know there's a raven living in the old barn?" Papa looked up from his plate. *That's a yes.*

"Really?" Mama sounded genuinely surprised. "I didn't think they lived in this part of the country. Just one?"

"I haven't done much research, but it's definitely a raven. And there's only one, which I know is a little odd. He scared me to death the other night."

"What were you doing in there anyway? That barn leans too much. It's dangerous." Dani couldn't help but feel that Papa was just trying to keep her out of there. *Too late, I've already got the envelope.*

"Oh, it'll stand a while yet," Mama said. *She must not know Papa's secret.* "Is there anything worthwhile still in there?"

"Just a couple tools and a nice workbench. I think the rest is trash, but I haven't looked that close. I think I'll pull that workbench out before the barn collapses." She glanced at her father, watching for his reaction. He didn't say anything. Didn't even nod or shake his head. But his jaw was clenched. That workbench was associated with something for him. Something he didn't want to acknowledge. For a long time, no one spoke. Mama seemed to realize that there was something more going on than a simple discussion of a workbench and a barn. She must have seen Papa's face, too, because she didn't ask.

"What's on your schedule tomorrow?" Dani glanced at her mother. Which one of them was he talking to? Mama didn't say anything, so Dani decided they must have already discussed whatever Papa had in mind.

"Nothing much. I need to go get groceries and a few supplies for work. What's up?"

"We need to work some pigs in the morning. Could use your help. If it's not too much trouble." It was an order, not an invitation. If she refused, he would make clear that she didn't really have a choice. But Papa preferred to rule mildly, through suggestion rather than commands. She decided to let him.

"Sure. I can be here. I'll come up right after chores. Moving them or just working them?" She prayed they were just working them. It would be much faster than having to work and then move the piglets. There would be new pens to prep, sows to move once their piglets were gone, and something always went wrong in the process of moving pigs.

"Just working them. I don't have a spot ready for them yet, so they'll stay put for a bit longer." Dani breathed a sigh of relief. She'd still have plenty of time to work on the house and finish her lit syllabus. Classes started in about a week, so she needed to get focused, even though classes hardly seemed important with the White Woman and the raven to figure out. Still, teaching was her income, so she'd better make sure she was ready. *Maybe we should read some excerpts from* The Woman in White. *It's too long for undergrads, but excerpts might be good. Might as well combine real life and teaching. Who knows, maybe rereading it will shed some light on JML.*

Armed with a pry bar and a ladder she'd had to awkwardly shove into her trunk, through the trunk's back seat opening, and all the way up between the front seats to bring home, Dani banged through her back door. The door caught on the bottom of the ladder. She jerked her shoulder forward to free it and slammed the top of the ladder into the wall.

"Oh good grief." She banged around a bit more before making the turn into the kitchen and over to the stairwell. She looked up the stairs at the landing, where she'd have to try to navigate the ladder around a 180 degree turn. The ceiling was high enough there, but still. Not tonight. She leaned the ladder against the wall and considered the pry bar in her hand. Her body ached, her hands especially. She could feel herself growing stronger here, but tonight she just wanted to rest. She dropped it next to the ladder. *Whiskey, read, bed.*

Upstairs, Dani checked the dresser drawer for the gun. Still there. She dug through her bag of books, hoping *The Woman in White* was one she'd saved. She hadn't been able to read since it happened, and she'd been in such a hurry that she wasn't entirely certain which books had made it into her car. *The Moonstone* surfaced, and Dani paused to study the cover, edged in yellow. It had been her first experience with Wilkie Collins and she'd fallen in love immediately. It might do if she couldn't find *The Woman in White*. It was even short enough that the undergrads might actually try to read it. She set it to the side and kept digging. The pile of discarded books grew. She'd managed to grab quite the assortment, from a few of her old *Hardy Boys* collection to Faulkner and even Picoult. To say she read widely would be an understatement. Now, though, there was only one book she wanted. Finally, her hands closed around an impossibly thick paperback. She pulled it into the light. The pale green cover of *The Woman in White* with a sour looking woman in a white dress glaring up at her. *Finally*. She rocked back on her heels and flipped open to a bookmark she'd left in it long ago. It had taken her three tries to read it all the way through. It was worth it.

Dani opened the book, holding it in one hand with her thumb and pinky propping open the pages. Whiskey in the other hand, she walked idly as she read. A bad habit. She'd run into more than her fair share of walls and furniture this way. But some books just required that you move as you read, or at least Dani thought so. She leaned against the doorway to the wrecked bedroom. At the end of the first page, she looked up. It would be awkward to turn the pages this way, thick as this book was. She wondered what JML would think of her choice of reading. Wondered, too, if she'd ever read it. Dani looked down at the first line again. "This is the story of what a Woman's patience can endure, and what a Man's resolution can achieve." Collins wrote the line more than 150 years ago, but he might as well have written that line about her own life.

"What did you endure, J? Was it your man, too, that you had to endure? Or something else?" The room was silent, not even falling plaster for Dani to interpret as J's attempt to communicate. She closed her book and tucked it under her arm. Tugging her phone from her pocket, Dani snapped a picture of her progress in the room to send to Kat. A white smudge appeared on the screen in between J's window and the other window on the far wall. Dani swiped at it with her thumb, but the mark remained. She zoomed in. It was part of the photo. *Hi, J. Nice to see you again. Oh good Lord, I'm friends with a ghost.* She sent the photo to Kat with a note about knocking down plaster. She didn't mention the ghostly smudge. Maybe she was losing it.

"Nice! Is that your ghost in the middle?" Well, if Dani was losing it, so was Kat.

"I think so. I've started calling her J. Seems weird for her not to have a name." Dani filled Kat in on her potential lead on information through Marie. She hoped Marie would text soon. As much as she hated to think of trying to keep Marie focused, it was her best shot at answers.

"Any more texts from him?" Kat's question sent chills rippling through Dani's body. A firefly flashed at J's window. She hadn't heard any more from him, but she kept waiting, expecting him to text, call, show up at her door. It wasn't like him to send one text and be done with it. When she'd hidden at Kat's for a time, he'd texted relentlessly and driven around looking for her until he found her car, parked at the very back of Kat's apartment complex. He was persistent, the bastard. So why was he giving up so easily now? Surely a divorce decree wouldn't have that much of an impact.

"No." Dani didn't have it in her to explain all that she was thinking and fearing right now. She wandered back to her bedroom and undressed. As she tugged her jeans down over her hips, she felt a crinkle. The envelope. She'd stuffed it into her back pocket and forgotten in her rush to leave the barn. No markings on the outside, other than the corner torn away by the raven. She slipped a nail under the flap. Sealed shut. Perched on the edge of the bed, Dani took a breath and ripped open the envelope. She reached inside. As she pulled out a single sheet of paper, her phone buzzed loudly on the wooden dresser. Dani jumped, heart pounding in her chest. It was him. Somehow, she knew this before she grabbed her phone.

"Living with your parents now? Or just visiting?" *How does he know? Lucky guess?* "That blue shirt you wore to church looked nice. Maybe I could come with you next week." She sat staring at the screen, unable to move. *Not a lucky guess. He wasn't there. Who does he know? How did he find out?* "I miss you." Dani's jaw clenched. Tonight, he was the kinder version of himself. The one that could fool people into thinking that she was the one who was evil. He'd certainly fooled their church leaders up north. But underneath the sickly sweet facade was a man desperately trying to regain control. She'd found that out after he'd fooled her the first time. Well, second time, if she was being honest. Now, this version of him just pissed her off. It was enough to get her moving again.

She screenshotted the messages and sent it to Kat. "Speak of the devil..."

"And he will appear. Is he right about church and the shirt or lucky guess? At least he doesn't know about your house."

"He's right. I have no idea how, but he knows." She flipped back to his messages. Responding would do no good. She knew that and yet...

"Do not answer him. We'll find out how he knows some other way." Count on Kat to read her mind.

"Right. I'm trading my car in for a pickup. Had to haul a ladder today and it got ridiculous. Plus, one less signal for him that I'm around." Decision made and nerves somewhat calmed, Dani retrieved the gun from her drawer, pulled back the slide to chamber a bullet, and set it next to her on the bed. If he was this close, she needed to be ready. She picked up the envelope again and dropped her phone to the bed, daring it to buzz again. Dani pulled out the single sheet of paper. It was plain white, just like the envelope. She tossed the envelope aside and unfolded the paper. The handwriting could almost have been her own. It matched that on the workbench perfectly. It was dated neatly in the top right corner. "5 August 1973" it read, the same year on the stone.

"If you find this, I'll be gone. You'll find my pistol under the bench. I couldn't take it with me. Not with her initials etched into it like a permanent memory. Take care of it. It's served me well. Everything else will be gone to hell in a hand basket by then, so do whatever you want with the rest.

You'll be wondering why. Why did I kill her? Why did I run off afterwards? I guess it's simple. I'm not right. Haven't been since I got home, but you can't tell people that. Not when other guys lost their legs or arms if they came home at all. But I can't sleep without dreaming. Sometimes I'm back there and it's awful, but it's familiar. I can handle that. I wake up sweating or shouting, but I'm okay. I know I get out alive. It's the other dream, the one she's in, that's driving me batty. I don't suppose it matters now, but for what it's worth, she's wearing a triangle straw hat tied under her chin, and she's wearing a white shirt and skirt. She looks just like the women we'd see in the rice paddies over there. In the dream, she looks at me and then just turns away and bends over to work in the paddy again. She doesn't seem to care that I'm there at all. I say her name, but she doesn't move. I run toward her. I grab her by the shoulder and spin her around, but her face is gone. It's the same bloody, pulpy mess Pete's was, but it's hers. I drop her in the rice paddy and run. That's when I wake up. Running from her. And I never feel bad, because she didn't care that I was there.

I have that dream a lot now. She doesn't care that I'm here when I'm awake. She acts scared of me. I know I've changed, but I'm her husband, damnit. Anyway, that's why. If you're reading this, then she's become the rice paddy woman in my dream and I couldn't take it any more. I've left so that you don't have to decide whether or not to defend me. I don't care if I get caught or go to jail. I did the thing. I should go away, probably for the rest of my life. But I'd rather it happened later, when the kids are older. Or maybe in a different state. I'll pay for what I've done either way, I promise. I'm not trying to escape that.

I love you all. I'm sorry.

Jake"

Dani read the note twice. So the JML etched on the grip stood for Jake's wife? There were still details to discover, but it seemed clear that the White Woman she'd been seeing had been murdered by her own husband. His explanation didn't make much sense, but then he was clearly suffering from PTSD. Nobody knew or talked much about it back then, though. He would have been on his own. Who had he hoped would find the note? In 1973, it would have been just her father and grandmother on the main farm. Grandpa had already passed and Papa hadn't been dating Mama yet. He would have only been in his early teens, if she remembered correctly. Jake had apparently had kids, but surely the note wouldn't have been for them. *Who were you writing to? How did you know he'd find it? I guess you didn't know. Pretty sure I was not your intended audience.* Dani looked absently toward the window overlooking the old barn. She couldn't see it from the bed, but she imagined the raven perched in its rafters, looking her direction.

She tucked the letter into *The Woman in White*, turned on her cell phone flashlight, and flicked off the light. She drifted off as a man in the book yelled to a policeman that a woman had escaped from the asylum. A woman in white.

~ 6 ~

Dani rolled over, batting at her phone to turn off the alarm. The sun had barely begun to light the sky and, after the text from him, she'd slept only fitfully, fighting off nightmares. She'd kept the gun on the floor and reached out to touch it when she woke from dreams of him creeping up the stairs to drag her back with him. She rolled over, but her phone went off again. This time, she picked it up to check the screen. This alarm read "Work Pigs." *Shit.* She'd forgotten. *No rest for the wicked.* She pulled on a pair of old jeans and a t-shirt she didn't care about. She tucked the gun back into her dresser drawer before heading downstairs for muck boots, praying she'd get to her parents' early enough to chug some coffee before work began. She rushed through morning chores and hopped into the car.

Dani was surprised to find her father still sitting at the kitchen table, nursing his coffee. *Don't look a gift horse in the mouth.* She pulled a mug from the cupboard and poured herself a cup. It had an oily look to it and she wondered how long it had been since he cleaned the pot. But coffee was coffee. She sat and sipped in silence with him. A few minutes later, she heard her mother enter the back porch from outside.

The click of cabinet doors opening and closing told her that her mother was preparing the tools they'd need to work pigs. Syringes, clippers, scalpels, bottles of medication, chalk, all piling into the work tray.

The door from the back porch into the kitchen swung open and Mama leaned in. "You two ready?" Papa finished his coffee in one swig and stood, stretching. *Is he getting old?* Dani chugged her coffee as well and headed back to the front door to retrieve her boots. She took a deep breath and realized that she was nervous. It had been a few years since she'd helped work pigs. What if she messed it up? *Dock the tail, clip the eye teeth, one shot on each side of the neck, probably two cc's unless the meds have changed, pass the boars to Mama to castrate, mark with the chalk, done. I got this.* After the first few piglets, she and Mama fell into a rhythm, dividing the work and moving quickly. Papa bounced between catching piglets for them, checking other pigs, and working some on his own. An hour later, shirt covered in blood, shit, and sweat, Dani stepped to the door of the barn for a break. They were almost done, and Mama needed to refill syringes anyway.

"I can get this last pen if you need to go." Dani turned to look back at Mama. "I know you want to go to the store and I'm sure you have work to do for school."

"I do, but I can finish this pen with you." Dani walked back in, caught a piglet, hooked her finger into its mouth and snagged the clippers. The faster they worked, the faster she could trade her car in and get the essentials. As she passed the piglet to Mama for castration, she contemplated her shopping trip. She'd take the gun. With him this close, she couldn't risk not taking it. But she'd have to leave it in the car. She didn't have a license, a holster, or any idea what it would take to legally carry it on her. Maybe she'd research some gun classes later, too. She snagged another piglet and wondered what kind of car she should get. What she'd told Kat was true, a pickup would be handy, but the gas mileage would suck. Although that wouldn't matter much if she kept working from home.

By the time they'd finished working the litter, Dani had a plan. She stopped in her parents' house to chug two big glasses of water and text Kat. "Hey, who do you know who could help me out with my concealed carry license?" The answer was quick, a guy who lived about a half hour away. With any luck, he'd respond to Kat's message today and Dani could start carrying all the time.

Back at home, Dani stepped into the downstairs bathroom. *Quick clean-up and on the road to check out some trucks and buy some coffee.* She scrubbed her hands again in the sink. Iodine was tough to get out, but this second scrubbing had her looking a little less like she'd just murdered someone. She turned off the tap and glanced in the mirror as she dried her hands. The sight stopped her for a moment. Then, she laughed. Staring back at her was a sweaty woman with frizzy hair and blood, shit, and God only knows what other bodily fluids covering her shirt. If he could see her now, he'd run the other way. She'd never have to worry about him again. She laughed until she cried, leaning on the pedestal sink. Finally, she recovered herself enough to take a picture to send to Kat.

"Good grief, woman, take a shower! Or at least fix your hair. You need to look cute to negotiate with those car salesmen." *Oh. Good point.* Dani wasn't about to take the time to shower, though. There was too much to do. She tugged her hair down out of its ponytail and attempted to reassemble it in a somewhat orderly fashion. It looked less frizzy than before, but it certainly wasn't going to help her get a good price on a truck. She took it down again, using some water to try to tame it. There. Wild, for sure, but presentable. She peeled off her clothes and scrubbed down with a wet rag. She'd consider a shower tonight, after she'd gotten even more gross. For now, she just needed to smell good. A fruity lotion helped to both revive her skin and cover the smell of hard work. Satisfied, she dropped her dirty clothes in the washer and started it before heading upstairs to find clean ones. Halfway up the stairs, she heard a sound, almost like whispering, coming from farther up. She froze, naked, on the stair landing. She had no weapon. Even her phone had been left in the downstairs bathroom. Seconds ticked by with no more sound. *Probably just the wind through that open window.* Finally, Dani decided to move. If he was up there, surely he would have heard her coming and made his move by now. He'd certainly be able to chase her down if she ran back down the stairs now, so she might as well take the fight to him, if that's what was happening. She crept slowly up the stairs, staying close to the wall. Even as she reached the top, there was no sound. *Maybe it was all in my head. I really am losing it.* Dani quickly scanned the hall and, deciding she was being ridiculous, went to work finding clean, semi-attractive clothing for her errands. She settled on a plain blue t-shirt. It wasn't fancy, but the color made her eyes pop, and her eyes were the only thing she liked about her appearance these days. A pair of jean capris that had to stretch mightily to go over her hips, flip-flops, and she was ready to go.

As she drove toward the nearest town, Dani realized she wasn't even sure which car dealerships were still around. Surely the old man who'd sold her her first car, a beat up old Pontiac, was gone by now. He'd seemed ancient back then, and that was more than ten years ago. *Should have looked up car dealerships. Idiot.* She slowed to 30mph at the city limits and decided to turn onto the main road, confusingly not named Main, and see what was there. She turned right at the grocery store and was thrilled to see that a car dealership had moved into the old Dairy Queen next door. There were even a few pickups on the lot. She pulled in and said a silent prayer that she'd find something good that she liked and would be a straight trade for her tiny car. The odds were not in her favor, but there was no harm in hoping.

Dani parked and walked quickly past the vehicles with five figure price tags on the windows. The cheaper used stuff would be at the back, she was sure. A salesman looked up from his desk as Dani got closer to the building. *Please don't come out yet.* He did anyway.

"Mornin'! Can I help you with something?" She almost felt bad for being irritated. He had a dad bod and seemed nice enough. Not sleazy like some salesmen. But there was still time. First impressions weren't everything, after all.

"Just looking." She saw him size her up, trying to guess at her budget and style. *Good luck, dude.*

"We've got some nice used SUVs over on the other side of the building." *So close, and yet so far.* "Are you wanting to trade?"

"Looking for a pickup. But yes, I do have a trade-in." She gestured back to her car. "It's locked, but you're welcome to look it over from the outside while I check these out." She nodded toward the pickups at the back of the lot. *Please, please, please do that.* This time, he seemed to hear her silent pleading.

"Sure. I'll meet you back there in a bit." He strode toward her car. Dani looked over a white pickup first. It had some body rust and a couple small dents, but it might work. The next contender was black with a big, boxy chrome grill and a lift kit. *No thank you. Save that for a man with something to compensate for.* A pale blue truck with a cream stripe down the body was next. It was by far the oldest, but she couldn't find any rust. Either it had been well taken care of or restored. The next two pickups were small, with short beds. Not her style. She turned back and contemplated the white pickup and the blue one. Maybe she ought to look over both. She popped the hood on the white one as the salesman rejoined her.

"If the inside of your car is as nice as the outside, we should be able to do a pretty good trade-in deal for you. I'm Richard." He stuck out his hand and Dani shook it. "This one may not look the prettiest, but it's in great shape. I figured I'd repaint her if nobody bought her soon." Dani ignored him, checking fluid levels and noting that he hadn't even bothered to clean up the engine bay. Odds were good that he'd just been hoping someone would take it off his hands before he sunk any money into it. She said nothing and stepped over to the blue truck.

"I was looking at this one, too. What's the story on it?" She popped the hood, impressed by the cleanliness of the engine bay, and began checking it over. Thank goodness Papa had taught her these things.

"Older guy sold it to us when he couldn't drive any more. It'd been in the family, he said. Seems to be in great shape, though the fuel mileage isn't what it would be in a newer truck." Dani nodded, but continued to stay silent. Her quick inspection told her the blue truck was by far the better value, gas mileage be damned. No sense in letting Richard know that yet, though.

"I'd like to test drive the white and the blue." They went into the office so he could copy her license and grab the keys. Thankfully, he was the only salesman working, so she got to drive alone. In return, she handed over the keys to her car so he could check it over more thoroughly. She called her cousin as she navigated the white pickup out of the lot. He was a mechanic and, though he didn't live here, he'd be able to offer advice based on the makes and models alone. He confirmed her suspicions: As long as both drove alright, the blue was the better bet. He also reminded her to check the wear on the tires, but said it wouldn't really change his mind. Decision made, Dani cruised down to the feed and seed store and turned around to head back to the dealership. She traded Richard keys and took the blue pickup out. It reminded her of her grandpa somehow, though he'd never driven a truck quite like this one. Maybe it was the bench seat, covered in a woven seat cover. Whatever it was, this truck felt right. When she pulled back into the lot, she braced herself. She certainly couldn't afford the $9,000 price tag, probably not even after her trade-in. She'd need to negotiate. Hard.

"So? What did you think?" Richard looked hopeful, and Dani wasn't quite sure if that was good or bad. "Do we have a winner?" He put his hands on his hips and his dad gut stuck out a little more. She smiled, cocking her hips to one side.

"Well, I think so, but a lot depends on my trade-in, of course. I'm starting over, so I can't really afford either of them." She was hoping the dad bod meant he'd have fatherly instincts. Risky, but her best move, since flirting didn't seem likely to work.

"Let's take a look at that trade-in." He sat down and gestured to a chair in front of his desk. He already knew the trade-in value. They both knew that. But this was just part of the dance. "We'll see if we can't make something work for ya." Dani looked around. He was still alone. There was no "we" here. Again, it was part of the dance. She wondered what he would do when they got to that point in negotiations where the salesman went in and pretended to argue with his boss to get the best deal and then came back out, mock triumphant, with the deal he'd already planned to offer anyway. "All right, so which truck were you more interested in?" Classic trick.

"I'd like to know the trade-in value first." She knew the question meant her trade-in was high. He frowned and clicked around on his computer, probably hoping she'd cave and tell him her preference. It wasn't happening. The blue truck was more expensive, and rightfully so. If he was smart, he'd low ball her trade-in based on the white pickup's price. If he wasn't, her job would be a lot easier. She'd asked her cousin about trade-in on her car, so she had a pretty good idea what range the salesman should be in. She didn't expect him to be even close.

"Looks like I can give you five for it." Dani laughed. He'd figured based on the white truck for sure, and fatherly instincts didn't seem to be working for her. Richard looked at her. "Maybe six." Dani started to stand up.

"I know what Kelley Blue Book is on it. I'll just go look elsewhere." She barely made it out of her chair before Richard responded.

"You know, I bet I can do better. Let me check some things." He went through a series of questions about her car's features and ownership. Things he already knew because he'd no doubt run the VIN while she'd been test driving. "Aha! Here we go. How does eight sound?" It sounded better than she'd anticipated and probably better than she deserved. That would only be $1,000 if she took the offer and paid sticker price.

"Sounds great. Now let's talk about that blue and cream pickup." Relief flooded Richard's face. He hadn't wanted to have to pay her for her car if she took the white one. "It'll need new tires sooner rather than later, and I think that left headlight is looking a little dim. What if we just knock it down to eight and call it a straight trade? The title's in my glove box." He probably already knew that. Had no doubt looked if he was a half-decent salesman. But still, no harm in emphasizing that this could be the simplest transaction he'd done in awhile. Richard leaned back in his chair, thinking, or pretending to.

"There will still be the fees, title work and all, but I think we could do that." They shook on it and Dani started transferring her few personal effects from her car to the pickup while he took care of the paperwork. A few signatures and a blessedly small credit card transaction later, Dani drove her new pickup a few hundred feet to park at the grocery store with a conveniently adjoining liquor store for a quick whiskey restock. *Today just might turn out alright.*

Driving home, Dani rolled her window down and blocked out the flapping of the plastic grocery bags by cranking up the country station her new radio had come pre-set to. It felt right. Easy. *Too easy.* She shook her head, as if to clear the anxiety, and sang along to the radio. She rounded a sharp curve, vaguely remembering that it had taken the life of a classmate one winter when it was icy. She couldn't recall his name, though, and that bothered her a bit. A little farther down the road was the site of her first ever car accident. Nothing major, but it stuck in her mind. She turned right at the corner where her high school best friend had told her that she'd lost her virginity to some guy from the next town over. This whole place was full of memories, things she hadn't thought about in years. They weren't all good, but being surrounded by familiar stories was comforting. This was her turf. Even if he was here, he was the one at a disadvantage. She smiled and pushed the pedal down a little more.

Her stomach was growling by the time she pulled into her drive, and Dani realized it was well past lunch time. She shoved her cold groceries into the fridge and freezer, leaving the rest on the counter to deal with later, and made a quick sandwich. She washed it down with a few Oreos as she headed upstairs to plan the rest of her day. Her classes were pretty much ready. She'd make an introduction video for them tonight, after she showered and looked human again, but otherwise there was nothing pressing there. *The Woman in White* did look tempting, lying there on her bed. But her own real-life woman in white was where Dani wanted to spend her time today. She stepped into the big bedroom and surveyed the work yet to be done. Today, she decided she would take down the trim, light switch, socket covers, and light fixture. That would clear the way for removing the rest of the plaster tomorrow. She'd need to talk to Papa about where she could dump it. Trash removal wasn't a thing this far out, and if plaster would burn at all, Dani doubted it would be fast or pleasant.

Having retrieved her pry bar, a screwdriver she'd found when cleaning out her car, and a tall glass of whiskey, Dani set to work. For now, she'd leave the trim on the floor next to where it had come from. Once it was all down, she'd go through and label it before moving it out of the way. The first couple pieces of baseboard came out easily. The third piece required a bit more elbow grease, a couple whiskey breaks, some carefully selected curses, and a cheer when it finally popped free. Dani sat on the floor, sweating. The baseboard was about six feet long so, tough as it had been, at least it had been worth it. She rose to her feet. The first window was up now. She hadn't fought with the ladder yet, so Dani slipped her pry bar under the trim to the left side of the window. She'd worry about the top later. It popped loose easily enough and she laid the board carefully on the floor. Next was the bottom piece, which came loose almost immediately. She studied the window ledge and decided she'd need to free the other side before working on it. Right side trim down, she knelt to slide her pry bar under the ledge and gently pushed up. At first, the wood just bowed. She jiggled the pry bar a little closer to the side and tried again. Less bowing this time, so she pushed harder. A satisfying "pop" sounded as the left side lifted. She grabbed the board and set it behind her with the others. A paper fluttered to the floor. An old photograph. She turned it over. There was writing on the back, but it was so faded that she couldn't make it out. In the picture, a black dog with long hair sat between a woman in a skirt and hat, slightly stooped over as if just standing up from petting the dog, and a man, tall and rail thin. A single story house stood behind them. The photo was old. Not only was it black and white, but the edges were scalloped. Her grandmother's scrapbooks had held some scalloped edge photos. She wondered when they were taken. She set the photo on the floor near the door and continued work, wondering if it had anything to do with her woman in white.

Dani had removed the bottom and side frames of three windows. She swiped some sweat from her forehead as she stood considering J's window, the next to tackle. Did she dare disturb the place where she'd seen her most often? "J, I promise I'm going to put everything back and make it pretty again, okay?" She wedged the pry bar under the first trim board and waited. All was still. *Here we go.* Dani set to work removing the board. The second side also came off without a hitch. *So close.* She began to work the pry bar under the bottom edge. *Did the room just get cooler?* A light breeze played with her hair as Dani looked around to see if the woman in white was there. Nothing. The breeze strengthened and a flutter caught her eye. *The picture.* Dani dropped the pry bar and ran to catch the picture before it disappeared down the hallway and into another room or even out another open window. It had made it to the top of the stairs before she snatched it up. Breathing heavily, Dani examined the writing on the back more closely as she walked back to J's room.

The loopy cursive was faded enough to be nearly illegible, but maybe, with careful study and maybe playing with some photo filters she could make it out. Was that the loop of a capital L? As she crossed the threshold of J's room, she felt the cool breeze and with it, a sense of dizziness. She looked up and saw the room as if through gauze. The bed and nightstands were back. The covers of the bed were rumpled this time, as if the sleepers had been suddenly called from bed in the middle of the night. Dani walked closer, feeling as if she were floating toward the bed. The drawer of the empty nightstand stood open. She angled toward it, curious to see if it, too, was empty. The air felt sticky and Dani looked to the window to find the heavy drapes pulled tightly closed.

No sign of any air movement. She turned back to the drawer. Inside was a familiar leather holster and three brass colored bullets. *Where is the gun?* She looked around the room, but there were no other furnishings, no other place someone might set a gun down. Only a wardrobe for hanging clothes, and she doubted she'd find a gun in there. *Maybe in the other nightstand.* She walked around the bed and reached for the drawer. *Can I touch things here?* The drawer pull felt solid under her fingers, though even her own arm looked hazy in this parallel world. She tugged the drawer open. A journal, pill organizer, and some pens. *What were you taking?* Dani picked up the pill box and shook it, rattling the contents. She popped open the Saturday slot. A small, round, orangey brown pill sat alone in the slot. *An organizer for just one pill?* She popped open Friday. Just one pill again. She fished the pill out of its slot. The wind whipped up. It got colder. Dani's hair flew in front of her face. She held the pill closer to her eyes, struggling to see the imprint. 136. The pill flew from her hands and the dizziness became overwhelming. Dani fell to the floor and suddenly, she was back in the torn up bedroom, sweating, not a breeze to be found.

    From her perch on the couch, laptop on her thighs, Dani stretched to reach the tall glass of whiskey on the floor. It had taken a cool sponge bath and quite a few swallows of whiskey to shake the anxiety brought on by the vision this afternoon. Vision. That's the word she'd settled on for naming the experience, but really it felt more like a parallel universe. Like the story was happening at the same time somehow. She felt like she was being watched. Some of it was suspicion that he'd found her, but now she wondered if some of the feeling was coming from inside the house, from another time entirely. For now, though, she focused on her teaching. Her courses were nearly built. She sipped her whiskey and then set it back down. Kat had texted earlier to ask how things were going, but she'd still been recovering from the vision.

"Things are good. Traded in the car, bought groceries, worked on that bedroom. Even took a shower." Dani hit send, wondering if she should tell Kat about the vision.

"A shower? Really?" She could almost see Kat's raised eyebrows.

"Well. Sort of. I wiped myself down with a cool rag. Same difference."

"No word from him or sightings of your woman in white?"

"Nope." *It's not technically a lie.* "I did find a cool picture while I was working." She told Kat about the picture and how she'd almost lost it in the breeze.

"Did you recognize the people in it?"

"No. Not the house, either, but I need to look closer." Dani shifted her laptop to the couch and went upstairs to retrieve the photo. She snapped a picture of it and sent it to Kat, then settled back in on the couch to examine it herself. The dog's ears stood upright and its nose was long and slender. It was looking straight at the camera. *Is he watching me, too?*

Dani's phone buzzed. Distracted by the dog's gaze, Dani glanced at her phone, expecting a message from Kat. Instead, a message from a number she didn't recognize was previewed on the screen. Frowning, she unlocked her phone.

"Hey, Dani, I can meet you at the shooting range sometime and we can check out the gun and I can go over the licensing basics. It's nothing too bad. When do you want to meet up?" *Oh, right, the gun guy Kat suggested.* She fired off a response basically indicating that she had no life and could meet around his schedule. They settled on the next afternoon, and Dani said a silent prayer that the gun range was indoors and air conditioned.

"What's the guy holding in his left hand? And is that a sheepdog?" Kat's text refocused Dani's attention on the picture.

"I think that's a shepherd's hook. There's one hanging in the barn. Not sure about the dog, but I'll look." Dani searched for long-haired black sheepdogs and within seconds, she'd found the one. "You're right, I think it's a Belgian Sheepdog." She sent a link to the AKC page on the breed.

"Safe to say they had sheep, then."

"I guess so. Why anyone would want those stupid creatures is beyond me. But the dog could be cute." There'd been no dogs or sheep yet in her visions. Maybe this photo was before or after her woman in white. Maybe it wasn't connected at all. She studied the photo again, focusing on the house in the background. *Only one story, so not this house. Or this house before it was built onto.* She couldn't see any other landmarks in the picture. Nothing that stood out to help her orient herself. The house was simple. No front porch, like the house had now. As far as she could tell, it was just a square house with no frills at all. It didn't even look like it had been painted, or else the paint had all worn off.

"Anything else exciting happen today?"

"Meeting up with that guy tomorrow."

"Corwin? Cool. He'll make sure you're all set."

"Yeah." Dani didn't hit send. More had happened. But should she share? Kat might well recommend a psychiatrist, and she probably wouldn't be wrong. This vision had been so real, so . . . tactile. As she continued to debate telling Kat what she'd seen, Dani searched for information on the pill she'd seen in the vision. She didn't have much to go on, but it turned out to be enough. Tofranil. 50mg. A little more searching revealed that her woman in white had been under psychiatric treatment, likely for depression. The pills had some nasty side effects, probably why it wasn't widely used anymore. The very first side effect listed, Dani was certain the woman had had: dizziness.

~ 7 ~

The heat woke Dani before her alarm. She tossed the thin sheet off of her and groaned. Her head was still fuzzy with a confused dream of him appearing in the room with the white woman, plaster raining down from the ceiling around the two of them as Dani watched them embrace from the doorway. She felt sick and turned away before the dream ended.

Dani pushed herself out of bed. She could already hear the calves lowing, asking where she was with their feed and carrots. Still, Dani moved slowly. Her sleep had been fitful and it was already far too hot. Her jeans stuck to her sweaty thighs, and if she hadn't been heading to meet Corwin for her gun lessons right after chores, she would have skipped struggling into her sports bra. At least she'd finally bought her own coffee. Dani stumbled down the stairs and started the coffee before grabbing a handful of carrots, tugging on her muck boots and heading out the door to the calves. A quick carrot delivery and nose scratch to each of the seven calves and she was headed to the pigs.

"Good morning, Anika." Dani shoved the white gilt out of her way with her knees and latched the door behind her.

"Get back in your pen if you want breakfast." Dani slid the hatches open on the feeders that needed topped off and stepped outside to flip the auger on. It was already muggy, but a light breeze helped. It also filled the air with pig feed, but you take the good with the bad. Papa usually went inside to finish checking pens and make sure he knew exactly when to turn the auger off or close off individual feeders. But then, Papa always had a mask and Dani couldn't seem to remember to grab one. She kicked at the rocks in the driveway while she waited. *I need to let Mama come help me tonight.* Mama really was trying, and having her help with the bedroom would mean uninterrupted time to talk about the stone, the woman, and what on earth Papa was hiding about this place. *I've also got to text Marie. She definitely knows something helpful if I can just get it out of her. And I've got to make sure I'm free to see Corwin this afternoon. How did I get so busy when I moved to the boondocks?*

Dani opened the barn door long enough to glance at the closest feeder. All good. She flipped the auger off and went back in to make sure all was well. Anika seemed to have taken her advice and gone back into her pen for breakfast. The first few pens were fine, if a little rowdy at the feeding troughs. In the third from last pen, though, Dani spotted her worst nightmare: a still, bloated, red-speckled pig. "Just what I needed," she muttered. She snagged the chain and handle off the wall of the barn and swung her legs over into the pen. Most of the pigs scattered at her entrance. They were little, relatively speaking, still under 200 pounds and skittish. Dani knelt to wrap the chain around the pig's back leg, above the joint. She felt the curious noses of the other pigs pressing against her back and arms. She hooked the handle through the chain and stood, making hissing sounds at the pigs to urge them away. She tugged. The pig's body didn't move. She leaned back away from the handle, digging her feet in and backing away from the pig. Gritting her teeth, she kept pulling. Finally, it budged. The movement was small but it was enough to get momentum going. She turned without ceasing the pulling movement. Digging her feet in like a runner at the starting blocks, she kept moving and soon the pig's body was at the gate. She swung it open and tugged him into the aisle while a few of his pen mates unceremoniously walked over him and pushed past her into the alley.

"Jerks," she yelled, though they didn't seem to pay her any mind. Once the body was removed, Dani unhooked the chain and hung it back up before chasing the escapees back into the pen and pulling out her phone.

"Hey, Papa. You've got a dead one in the finishing barn. I pulled him into the alley." She hung up after Papa assured her that he would take care of the rest. *Shoot. Should have asked him what to do with all that plaster I'm knocking down.* She called Mama instead.

"Hi, Mama. I wondered if you'd be available to help me knock down plaster tonight." As her mother detailed her plans for the day, Dani wandered toward the house, ducking her head into the barn to say a silent hello to the raven on her way. He cocked his head at her as if she were crazy, and she was pretty sure he was right. As she pulled frozen waffles from the freezer, Mama said yes, she thought she could help tonight. "Awesome. I'm headed to Osage this afternoon but I should be home before chore time, so we can do it after supper when it's cooler." Mama agreed and Dani hung up, feeling like she'd accomplished quite a lot before 9am.

Plate piled with passably edible blueberry waffles but no syrup, another grocery error she'd need to remedy soon, Dani plopped onto the couch and flipped open her laptop. She scrolled Facebook idly while she ate, but was bored before the first cardboard waffle was gone. She clicked over to her classes, checked enrollment numbers, and ensured that her finished syllabi were published. Just the literature syllabus to finish. She opened the unfinished syllabus document. Luckily, it was mostly a form from the department, but she still needed to nail down a few readings and one last writing assignment before she could publish.

"The lit syllabus is always the hardest," she said aloud. The thump of falling plaster came from upstairs. Dani's gaze flew to the ceiling. "Okay, just because I'm talking out loud doesn't mean I'm talking to you. And what do you care about my syllabus anyway?" Another thump. "I'll come see you soon. Just wait." Dani finished eating, typed a quick note about a ghost investigation for the final literature course paper, and took her plate to the sink. She leaned against it, enjoying the view of the leaning barn, the calves at the old dairy barn, and the open expanse beyond.

Dani's phone buzzed, startling her. She pulled it from her pocket to find a message from Corwin. "Are we still on for 1 today?" She texted back in the affirmative and started to put her phone away when she remembered Marie. She wasn't in the mood for a phone call, so she decided to hope that the number Marie had given her was a cell.

"Hey, Marie! It's Dani. I'm living in your old house. I have an unexpectedly free morning if you want to swing by to see it. Sorry it's such short notice!" Dani said a silent prayer that Marie also had no life and would be free to come provide some answers as she slid the phone in her pocket, refilled her coffee cup, and headed upstairs to work. As she set her coffee cup on the upstairs bathroom vanity to protect it from the plaster dust, she surveyed the bathroom. The long wall of the shower had been stripped down to the lathe for some reason. The other two shower walls bore the familiar cheap white plastic shower walls that she'd grown up with. The tub was stained, or at least filthy, and a crumbling yellowed stopper dangled from the faucet. She shuddered. This needed to be her next project, if only because it would allow her to take baths.

"Alright, J, I'm here. Let's get to work." Dani pulled her bandanna over her nose and began prying trim away from the windows before knocking plaster loose. She'd cleared two more windows before she stopped for coffee. The work was quicker now that her hands had calloused and she'd developed a plan. As she sipped, she checked her phone. Marie had answered.

"Yes! I can be there in about fifteen minutes. If that's okay. Let me know if not. Otherwise I'll head your way. I can't wait!!!" Dani groaned inwardly at the multiple exclamation points. This was going to be rough. Marie better know something worth knowing. She texted back that she was excited to hear about the house and turned to go back to work.

"J, we're about to have company and I'm gonna need you to be nice about it." Dani swung the hammer, sending plaster cascading to the floor just as a chunk fell from the ceiling directly behind her. "Hey!" She put her free hand on her hip. "J, that's enough. She knows something about this house. Maybe she can help us." There was no answering plaster, so Dani assumed J must be at least thinking about this idea. She turned back to the wall she'd been finishing and kept working. One last piece of trim to pull, and it was on the floor, so it would be easy. Then it would be time to get the ladder and finish the tops of the walls and the ceiling. Although, if she kept making J mad, there wouldn't be much left to remove.

As Dani grunted, feeling as if she was losing a fight with the last trim piece, she heard a voice. "Hello? Dani? Are you here?" *Marie.* She'd nearly forgotten about her. Had it really been fifteen minutes already?

"Up here!" She gave one last yank and heard the nails groan as they slid free. She landed unceremoniously on her rear as the trim clattered to the floor and a cloud of plaster dust rose around her.

"Oh, my! I see you're renovating this room. Just so beautiful. This was our playroom." Dani looked around through the haze of dust. *Beautiful?* She hoped Marie was talking about what it used to look like. Otherwise, she was already raising serious doubts about her credibility.

"We had this giant toy box right here in this corner, and a doll house over here. The bookshelf was on this wall by the door. We loved to lay on this big circle rug in the middle of the room while we played Barbies." Marie spun around slowly, as if seeing it all again. "This room was my favorite." The words had all tumbled out so fast that Dani was at first confused by the silence.

"Why did you love it so much?" Marie stood staring toward J's window. She still didn't seem to see what was really in front of her, but what had been. After a moment, she turned and smiled at Dani, still sitting on the floor.

"It was the only room that was ours. We had fun here. We fought here, too, of course, like sisters do. But this room was always cool in the summer and so we hid from work here all the time." She giggled.

"Didn't they find you here? It's not like you were really hiding very well."

"Oh, of course. But Dad didn't like coming in here much. I think that's why we got this room and they took that smaller bedroom downstairs." She frowned. "Mom didn't love it, either, but she would come in. She always wanted us to keep the windows shut, though. She said Dad shouldn't have given us a second story play room. I supposed we did occasionally drop a toy or two out the window," she giggled again, "so I can see her point."

"Why didn't your dad like it?" *It was cold back then, too. I guess that makes sense, since J would have already been here.* "This would have been the perfect master bedroom."

"You know, I'm not sure." For once, Dani was thankful that Marie loved to talk, because she would no doubt talk herself into an answer. "At first he said he wanted that downstairs bedroom so they'd be close enough to the stairs to know if we snuck out. But we could have crawled out our windows onto the porch roof, so I don't think that was it." She paused, looking around the room again, then back at Dani. She opened and closed her mouth a few times, as if deciding exactly what to say. "Mom didn't like it, but Dad did believe the house was haunted back then. I'm sure he doesn't believe that now, of course. Mom got him to start going to church, so I think all of that got fixed. But back then I think he thought it was haunted. He wouldn't go in that play room for sure, and I don't know of any other reason not to."

"Wow." Dani tried her best to put on a shocked face. "Did he ever say why he thought it was haunted? Surely he wouldn't have let you play in here if he really thought it was dangerous?"

"Oh, I never thought of that. I know the coolness of it bothered him. But that's all I know. He never said anything else to me about why he might not want to go in there. I just figured it was the mess we always had in there. Dolls everywhere, crayons, it was ridiculous. Definitely not what any parent wants to see, but they never made us clean it, really. It helped that they never came in to see it. Sometimes we'd go to bed and leave the door open. It was always closed in the morning, so I know they hated seeing it." Marie giggled at that, still enjoying getting away with the mess. "And I guess sometimes our dolls would be lined up on the windowsill, so Mom must have braved the room sometimes."

"Sorry, the windowsill?"

"Yes. I found it odd that she didn't put them in the dollhouse or the toy box, but I guess it was better than the floor. I'd come in some days and find them all lined up there, as many as would fit on the sill." Marie gestured toward J's window with her chin.

What were you playing at, J? Trying to get the girls to go to the window? Were you putting them in danger or keeping them safe? Or just having fun? Marie moved toward the door, prattling on about some ancient memory. Dani turned to follow, half-listening, when she caught a firefly flash of light out the window. *Having fun or keeping them safe, then. Maybe both.*

An hour and countless pointless stories later, Dani had finally dragged Marie outside, one step closer to her car. She'd had to exit the front door, though, to hear Marie's story about how her father had once fallen asleep in his rocking chair there and awoken to a raccoon stealing the fork from his abandoned dessert plate. At least that one was amusing. As they walked around the front of the house, they passed the rock inscribed with "1973 JML" and Marie stopped dead in her tracks.

"What is that?"

"The rock? I'm not sure. I found it but haven't found any answers yet. Why?"

"It's just. My sister. She had a, umm, a friend. Imaginary, obviously. No one lived around here. This spot was always covered in these really tall flowers. I didn't know this rock was here. Was it here back then?"

"I have no idea. I was hoping you could tell me. So who was your sister's friend?"

"Oh. I mean. Just imaginary. She was always telling me what she was doing and I got in trouble once for sitting where she was. Just silly little girl things. I just wondered because of the initials. I feel like most imaginary friends have silly names. Bobo or Dixie or the like. And you get to name your imaginary friend, right? I mean, I never had one, but it makes sense that you'd get to name it." Dani nodded and bit her tongue to keep from screaming at Marie to get to the point. "But she always said that her friend *told* her what her name was. Isn't that ridiculous? What kind of imaginary friend tells you their name?" Dani resisted telling her that she was pretty sure that wasn't all that weird. "Anyway, I'd forgotten all about her until I saw those initials. I mean, whose imaginary friend has a first, middle, *and* last name?"

Dani couldn't take it anymore. Her hands were balled into fists. "What was her name?"

Marie looked startled. "Sorry, I didn't know you'd care. Jilly Marie Lind. Are you okay? You seem kind of tense. I'm sure the imaginary friend has nothing to do with the rock. It was silly to think so. I just could not pass up that coincidence without telling you." She walked on, apparently forgetting the whole thing. "Is that barn new? I don't remember it, but then I wasn't outside all that much. It looks newer." She turned the corner to the other side of the house, Dani trailing behind in a daze. "Oh, now that barn I remember. Dad worked in there some, but he didn't like it. It was leaning even then. I think he was afraid it would fall on him. And there were birds. He hated birds. There was one that he said would hop down on the workbench and get in his way.

Wouldn't go away even when he tried to shoo it off. That bird wasn't afraid of anything."

Dani snapped to attention. "Sorry, did you say something about a bird?"

"Was I talking too fast again? Sorry, that's a bad habit of mine. I should really slow down but my brain just goes so fast sometimes. Yes, Dad talked about this black bird that would hop onto the workbench and refuse to leave no matter what he did. Dad was the one who would give up eventually and leave. I remember he set up a makeshift bench across sawhorses in the backyard instead. Mom thought he was being dramatic, but I don't blame him. Birds are gross."

"Right. Gross." Dani was back to half listening. *So the bird was here back then, too. And maybe trying to tell her dad something even back then. I wonder how long he's been trying to get someone to see what's going on here. What* is *going on here?*

When she tuned back in, Marie was talking about bird flu. Definitely worth interrupting. "Well, this has been super helpful. Thank you so much for filling me in on some of my home's history. I can't wait to get it all restored."

"Of course! Thank you for letting me reminisce. I know I can talk a lot sometimes, but you're a good listener. I hope you get it all done. I'd love to come see it when you're finished. Are you going to restore the dairy barn, too? I know there are cows there now, but it would be so cool to have it all back together. I guess you won't be able to save the barn, though. It's leaning so bad. That is so sad. I wish it had been better taken care of." Dani opened Marie's car door for her, hoping she'd get the hint. "Oh, thank you! You should really get a dog. That would just be perfect out here. Every farm needs a dog, don't you think? Maybe a big - " Dani shut the door and waved. Marie's mouth was still moving as she started the car and Dani walked away. She wondered how her conversation would end, and she found herself agreeing that a dog would be the perfect addition.

There was lots to think over from Marie's visit, so Dani hauled the ladder upstairs and set to work. It was easier to think when her hands were busy. She'd cleared all of the walls and part of the ceiling by 11:30am.

"Okay, J. I need to go shower so I can take this gun to Corwin and see what I can learn. We're almost ready to clear this out and start repairs, though. It'll feel more like home for you soon." A chunk of plaster fell from the ceiling. "Not sure if that means you're mad or excited. Either way, it's happening. See you soon."

Corwin was not what Dani was expecting in Kat's "gun guy" recommendation. "Are you sure this guy knows guns? He's wearing a flowery paisley shirt..."

Kat texted back immediately. "Yes, I promise. I know he's different. Just go with it. You'll like him."

"If you say so." Dani stuffed her phone into her back pocket and turned back to Corwin, who was patiently waiting and clearly knew he'd thrown her off.

"Well, let's see this gun." Dani couldn't quite place his accent. She pulled the gun out of its paper bag home and set it on the counter of the gun range. Corwin had paid their fees and secured new ammunition for her gun. They stood in the shooting gallery area now. Dani felt awkward, uncertain what to do. She'd wielded guns before, but mostly shotguns and never in this setting. He dumped the old ammunition out and began cleaning the gun with a kit he'd borrowed from the range owner. Dani made a mental note to ask him to teach her how to do this later. She wasn't surprised to see his rag covered in grime. After all, the gun had likely been under the bench since the 70s. Cleaning complete, Corwin reloaded the gun with the new ammunition and snapped the clip into place. Corwin had picked up ear protection for them, even though they were the only two on the range and Dani felt pretty certain it was unnecessary. Still, she followed his lead and donned the oversized headphone contraption when he did.

"I'll teach you how to clean and care for this later. Right now, let's make sure she shoots straight." Corwin demonstrated the proper grip and stance. "This is a heavy gun, so you won't be shooting it one-handed like you see in the movies." *Wanna bet?* Dani thought. *I definitely have to try it now.* Corwin fired a few shots. The first hit the target at the upper left edge. He adjusted his aim and the next two hit near dead center. "Alright, so she shoots a little high and to the left, so keep that in mind when you aim." He handed the gun over to her.

Dani took it, acutely aware that someone was watching her handle it this time. She took careful aim, then adjusted down and to the right. She took a slow breath in and squeezed the trigger, just as she'd seen Corwin do. Nothing happened. She squeezed a little harder. Still nothing. She felt her face going red. She couldn't let Corwin see her fail at this. This was *her* gun, after all. She felt a tap on her shoulder and turned to see Corwin grinning.

"What?"

"You might have better luck if you take the safety off." Dani felt all the blood rush to her face. She turned away from Corwin and flicked the safety, determined not to let him see her embarrassment. She aimed again. This shot needed to be perfect to make up for her mistake, but she couldn't seem to get her heart to slow down. *Damn anxiety.* She took several slow, deep breaths and squeezed the trigger. The gun bucked and she stumbled back half a step. She felt Corwin's arm around her shoulders and pulled away.

"Sorry. You okay? You did good, almost hit the center."

"Thanks," she mumbled, trying to brush off the anxiety his touch had sparked. Her shot wasn't quite as accurate as his, but it was better than she'd expected.

"You just need to put your foot back a little more and keep your core tight. Then you'll be perfect." Dani tried again. This time, she knew what to expect and felt more in control. Her shot wasn't any more accurate, but she didn't stumble back into Corwin, so she counted it a win. Half an hour later, she was getting better and Corwin had taught her how to clean the gun. She knew it was time to leave, but being out of the house and doing something that made her feel strong was addictive. She wanted to stay all day. And Corwin didn't smell half bad, either, even if he wasn't her physical type.

"I think you've pretty much got this down," Corwin said. "How about we go get you some ammo and a cleaning kit to have at home and maybe a holster if you want to carry that thing. Just at home, though. You don't need a license, strictly speaking, but I'd rather you took a class first." Dani nodded, sad that it was ending but knowing they both had other things to do.

Loaded up with supplies, Dani walked to the car with Corwin. She placed her bag in the back seat and turned back to Corwin. "Thank you so much. I feel better knowing how to use that thing properly."

"Any time. Any friend of Kat's is a friend of mine. Say, there's a cute coffee shop down the street. Want to go grab a midday snack?"

Dani felt her jaw drop and snapped it shut. "Me?"

Corwin laughed. "Well, yes. I don't see anyone else around. They make a killer turtle brownie."

"I don't like nuts." She felt the color rising in her cheeks. "I mean in my chocolate. I don't like nuts in my chocolate."

"They make other things, too." Corwin was clearly enjoying this.

"Oh. Okay. I mean yes. Sure. Let's go." Corwin chuckled and led the way to the coffee shop.

Dani's phone vibrated in her pocket. She pulled it out to find three messages from Kat. "Are you still at the range?" Then, five minutes later, "Yup. You are. I just checked. Hope it's going well!" The most recent text read "Are you going to the coffee shop with him?!?!"

Dani answered quickly, keeping an eye on Corwin as she did. "Yes, why? How do you know? Stop stalking me!"

"Because I can see your location, Jo. Duh. Do you think he's cute?"

"Are you seriously trying to set me up right now? He's too old for me anyway. His hair is already thinning." She hit send just as she collided full force with Corwin's chest.

"Oh shit. Sorry. I mean shoot."

Corwin laughed. "We're here." She saw that he was holding the door to the coffee shop open. "After you."

"Thanks," Dani found herself mumbling again. She ducked into the coffee shop and stopped. It was like a new world. There were plants hanging from a trellis above her head with Edison bulb lights woven among them. Overstuffed chairs circled a coffee table to one side. A long wooden counter held a plethora of pastries. Wooden tables with mismatched chairs filled the rest of the space. "Whoa."

"Right? I love this place." He stepped past her and up to the counter, surveying the pastry options. "Hey, Laurie," he greeted the waitress, "I'll take a turtle brownie."

"Sure. Here or to go? Your table is open." She nodded toward a grey table surrounded by a mixture of wooden chairs. A Scottish Highland cow painting hung on the wall above the bench seat on one side of the table.

Corwin looked at Dani, who shrugged. "Here is good. What do you want? I know you don't like nuts." He grinned at her and she made a face.

Laurie mock glared at Corwin. "Be nice. We have a delicious caramel brownie. Want to try that?" Dani nodded, grateful for the assist. Her phone buzzed and she glanced down at it. Kat.

"He's like six months older than you or something. A year max. Totally acceptable. DO IT!" Dani rolled her eyes.

"Anything to drink?" Dani fished her wallet out.

"Just water, thanks." She felt pretty certain a coffee shop wouldn't serve whiskey and it was too late in the day for her to want coffee. Especially given how Corwin had her nerves all in a tangle already.

"It's on me." Corwin handed his card to Laurie before she could object.

"I'll warm these up and bring them to your table," Laurie said with a smile.

Dani followed Corwin to his table and chose a seat across from him. *My age? Really?* "So Kat didn't tell me much about you, except that you could help with the gun."

"That sounds like Kat. I farm. Got a few of these," he gestured to the cow painting behind him. "Mostly crops, though. I grow pumpkins and sell 'em around Halloween. Corn, most of which the cows eat. The usual. What about you?"

"I teach college English online. And I guess I help my parents farm now. Cows and pigs. Papa does crops, too, but I don't do much with that." Laurie slid a warm plate in front of her. Dani picked up the fork and tried a small bite. "Oh my gosh. That is amazing."

"Laurie's good at what she does." Corwin took a bite of his own brownie.

"She bakes these? Dang." Dani took another bite. "This might need to become a regular stop."

"So I take it you're from around here if you're helping your parents and close enough to come over so I could teach you about your gun?"

"Yeah, just about half an hour east of here. I went to high school in Kaxe."

"I went to school here in Osage. Graduated in 2008."

"Hey, me, too! Small world."

"Not so small when Kat is orchestrating it." Corwin chuckled.

"So true. She is always scheming, isn't she? But I love her. She's been amazing to me this past year." Dani ducked her head and took another bite of brownie. Corwin didn't need to know everything about her.

"She's a good friend. Been a rough year, huh?" Dani looked up at him. Kat clearly trusted him. Should she?

"I guess. I'm home now. Working on fixing up an old house that's been in the family but abandoned for quite awhile. Just about done knocking the plaster down out of one room."

"Been there, done that. The house I live in was rough when I bought it. Had to knock down quite a bit of plaster myself. I'd love to show it to you sometime. And I'd be happy to give you some tips for your own house if you want. I love working on old houses."

Did he just invite me to his house? I wish I could text Kat and ask if he's safe, but I can't do that with him watching. Shoot. It's been quiet too long. "Oh. Umm." Corwin chuckled. *He laughs a lot. I like that.*

"I know you just met me. I didn't mean today. But eventually, I'm here if you want."

"Noted. I'm sure I'll need the help. And I've never seen a Scottish Highland in person."

"Really? They're sweet. Well, the two I keep as pets are anyway. They love to meet people. The teachers bring their classes out to pick pumpkins in October and the girls get lots of scratches from the kids." Dani smiled and felt herself relax.

"I bet that's cute."

"I think so. In another life, I might have been a teacher. Not sure I'd want to put up with the parents, though. They're something else." Corwin shook his head. "One mom came along with her kid's class and asked me if I could keep her son away from pollen. I said, 'Lady, we are on a farm. He'd need a bubble.'" He laughed. "I don't think she liked my answer much, but her kid seemed to have a good time."

Two hours and a coffee later, Dani was feeling an odd combination of energized and relaxed. She might regret the caffeine later, but they had to buy something and she sure didn't need another brownie. "I should really get back home and do some work," she said, but she made no move to get up.

"Yeah, there's plenty needs done at the farm." Corwin didn't move, either. He drained his coffee and smiled. His left front tooth was a little crooked and Dani smiled back. "I think this is the beginning of a beautiful friendship."

Dani laughed. "Isn't that a movie line?"

"*Casablanca.* You haven't seen it? What is wrong with you? I thought we could be friends," Corwin put a hand to his chest in mock shock.

"Well, maybe you'll have to introduce me to it sometime." Dani froze, staring down at her empty coffee cup. *Why did I say that? I barely know him. That was awkward.*

"Maybe I will." The invitation hung in the air until Laurie came to check on them.

"Need anything else, guys?"

"No, I really should get home," Dani pushed her empty cup toward Laurie. "Thank you so much." Corwin stood, placing a few ones on the table.

"Thanks, Laurie. Good to see you again." Laurie ducked her head as she took their cups and Dani caught the hint of a blush on her cheeks.

Corwin held the door and Dani stepped back out into the real world. "She likes you, ya know."

"Who? Laurie?" Corwin seemed genuinely puzzled.

"Yes. Pretty obvious if you ask me."

"Hmm. Guess I hadn't noticed. I'm not exactly looking anyway." They walked in silence, but Dani felt what she could only describe to herself as a warm hum between them. Corwin might be right. This might indeed be the beginning of a beautiful friendship.

Back at home, Dani called the dumpster company her father had suggested, checked in on her classes, tossed in a load of laundry, and did chores early. Tonight, she needed to call Kat.

~ 8 ~

Dani poured a glass of whiskey while Face Time rang. By the time Kat picked up, Dani was beginning to think that she was busy. Kat's face was red and her hair tousled when she answered.

"Gym or sex?" Dani bit her tongue to keep from laughing.

"Gym. Stair climber. Fly boy is history, remember? What's up?" Kat resumed her workout, huffing out words between exertions. "Did you meet up with Corwin?"

"What about rodeo guy? This is weirder than talking to you during sex. Yeah, I did. I learned how to take care of the gun, which is awesome. It's not so hard, now that I saw how."

"You could have learned online, ya know. But I'm glad you met Corwin."

"I know. But I do better hands on. Teaching online is hard enough without asking me to learn something, too."

"Fair. What'd you think of Corwin?" Dani knew halfway through what the question was, but she waited out Kat's breaths. It gave her time to think.

"He's nice. Had no idea the waitress at the coffee shop likes him, so maybe a little clueless. But nice."

"Wait. Coffee shop? I thought you were going to the range?"

"We went after the range. You know this. You stalked me, remember? He asked and you know I like coffee and chocolate. They have amazing brownies."

"Right. He pay?" Kat's shortening sentences were evidence that her workout was nearing an end.

"Maybe. But it wasn't a date. He was just being nice. Stop it." Even sweating profusely and red-faced, Kat managed to give Dani her signature "You're a moron" look. "I promise. I was sufficiently awkward to keep him from thinking anything of the sort." *Except that you told him you want to watch Casablanca with him.*

"Right. Don't believe that. He is clueless, though. Might not have noticed. You meeting again?"

"No. We didn't set anything up. I got the gun info I need, so I don't see why we would."

"Because single. Duh." Dani rolled her eyes. "And your ghost."

"What?"

"Ghost. Corwin knows history. And people. And believes in ghosts. Could help." Kat climbed off the stair machine and wiped her face with a towel. She grabbed the phone, putting it close to her face, "Call. Him."

"If I get stuck I absolutely will. But I won't. Marie gave me some good stuff to work with. And there's still Mom. She might know something."

"Wait, what did Marie give you?"

"A name. Apparently, my ghost's name is Jilly Marie Lind and she's been here quite a while."

"How did Marie know her name?"

"She didn't exactly. She didn't even believe in ghosts. But her sister's imaginary friend was named Jilly Marie Lind. Their parents avoided the room because it was cold, but sometimes they would go in in the morning and their dolls would be lined up in the window that JML is always at. She didn't know it, but JML was definitely there."

"Jilly. I don't know. I was hoping for a stronger name."

"What's wrong with Jilly?"

"Nothing, just sounds like a little girl, not a full grown woman."

"Hmm." Dani wandered into J's room. Jilly's room, she reminded herself. "I should tell you something." Dani filled Kat in on the visions. "She was a reader," Dani walked to the area where the bedside table had been. Would be again. "Do you think I'm crazy?"

Kat's eyebrows were drawn together. "Crazy? No. Stressed and drinking too much whiskey? Always. But full on crazy? No. I think she's real and she's showing you things for a reason. You're just the first person with enough crazy to listen."

"Thanks?"

"For real. It takes a special person to tune in to that kind of thing. Marie couldn't."

"Marie doesn't stop talking long enough to hear a spirit." Dani laughed. "Jilly probably stopped trying pretty early on. No way Marie was going to hear a damn thing."

Dani grabbed a whiskey refill and a cheese stick from the fridge before crashing on the couch. She talked with Kat for a while longer, just catching up. It was nice to laugh with a friend again. When they hung up, Dani sat in her now darkened living room, sipping her whiskey and staring at the TV. It was no use turning it on when it would only show static, but she didn't particularly want to get up to fetch her laptop or her book. Finally, Dani downed the last swallow of whiskey and stretched.

At the top of the stairs, she turned toward Jilly's room. "Jilly, I think we might just be okay here." There was no answering thump or flash. "I know you're probably not so sure about that. It's okay. I'm sure. We're going to be happy, Jilly. I promise." Dani moved slowly as she brushed her teeth and undressed for bed. She opted to clean up with a rag. No need to tempt her brain to unpleasant flashbacks after such a good day. When she dropped into bed, sleep came easily and, for the first time in a long time, she smiled as she slept.

Wednesday dawned hot but clear, and Dani silently thanked God for the lower humidity. After chores, she spent some time making videos for later assignments in her courses. If her mother had taught her anything, it was to work ahead, and Dani had been grateful for that lesson many times. After her third attempt to record a coherent explanation and demonstration of proper citation, Dani decided that she'd done enough working ahead for the day and slammed her laptop shut.

"Who the hell came up with the word parentheses anyway?" she grumbled to herself.

Dani stood and stretched, then wandered to the kitchen to dig for a mid-morning snack. She had plenty of time to make progress on the bedroom today, but her body was screaming for a break. Going from a soft city girl back to her country roots was taking its toll. It felt good, in that odd way that pain resulting from positive changes did, but a rest day would be nice. She surveyed the fridge contents and shut the door, not finding anything appealing. Her search of the cabinets wasn't any more successful. She chugged a glass of water and then wandered upstairs, hoping to find an excuse to do anything but knock down plaster.

In her room, Dani set to unpacking her bags. She made stacks on the floor of books, clothes, and keepsakes. She shoved the empty bags onto the top shelf in the closet and turned around to survey the mess she'd made. *At least now I can see what I have.* She picked up a blue-framed painting and traced the subject with her finger. A woman clutching at Jesus's robes and his tender hands holding her. *"...when the sacred is torn from your life and you survive..."* Dani swayed to the rhythm of the song that had come, unbidden, to her mind. She propped the painting up on the dresser and saw the scalloped edged photo. Still hearing the song in her head, she sat on her bed to examine the photograph more closely. Yesterday had been so busy she'd nearly forgotten it existed. There were no further clues in the image. Dani still thought it was her woman in white, but she couldn't be sure. She turned the photograph over in her hands and studied the writing again. Surely the writing held names and a date, but she still couldn't make them out.

Dani grabbed her cell phone and took a picture of the writing. She hit the edit button and scrolled through the filters offered in hopes that one of them would darken the writing enough to make something magically visible. A couple of them made the writing a bit more visible, but not enough to make it legible. She played with exposure, contrast, and a few other settings she didn't understand. No luck. *Probably because I have no idea what I'm doing.* Still, she kept fiddling with settings in hopes of lucking into something. Then she remembered that Kat had said that Corwin knew people.

"What are the odds you know somebody with some photography skills?" She figured Corwin had plenty of other things to do, but hoped he wouldn't wait too long to respond. She didn't want to do any of the other things she needed to do, and pursuing the photograph would be a welcome distraction. She was arranging her books by genre in stacks next to the dresser when her phone buzzed. Jody Picoult's *Between the Lines* had just been nestled into a spot all by itself, defying easy categorization and being the only romance in her small collection.

"Depends. What do you need exactly? What are we taking pictures for?"

"Sorry, not taking pictures. I have an old photograph with some writing on the back that I can't read. I want to try to restore it."

"Ah. That's a whole different question. Shoot me some pictures of it and I'll check around." Dani sent him pictures of the front and back. "Perfect. I'll forward these to Sarah first and see what she says."

"You rock!" She stared at the phone, willing herself to think of something better to say. Something to keep the conversation going. *Nope, Dani, you have plenty to do here or you can have a lazy day. Don't be awkward.* She hit the send button and tucked the phone into her pocket. She stepped out of her room and examined the bedroom across the hall. The carpet needed pulled up for sure. Dani let her hand trail along the wall as she walked the perimeter of the room, studying the walls and ceiling. No signs of water damage here. The popcorn ceiling was less than ideal, but the room seemed solid enough. At least she could leave the plaster up here for now, if she wanted.

Dani spent the rest of the day drifting between reading, studying the house, and adding to her growing list of home projects. Her phone buzzed, but she ignored it. Today was for her. A mid-afternoon nap left her aching body feeling a bit stiff, but refreshed. She checked her phone, but saw nothing urgent and tucked it back into her pocket. After chores and supper, Dani cocooned herself in her room and read. For once, sleep came easy.

"Okay, what are we doing today?" Dani consulted her master list of to-dos and chewed on the end of her pen. She'd already written "Morning chores" on her list for the day and crossed it out. A review of the messages she'd ignored yesterday had revealed that Corwin did have a friend who could help, but she'd need the actual photograph. A quick trip to Osage could be fun. Corwin had said to just let him know when she wanted to bring the picture over, so maybe today would work. She shot him a quick text to see and jotted

"Photograph?" down on her list. She added "Knock down plaster" while she waited for a response. As nice as yesterday's break had been, Dani knew she would have time and needed to make progress.

"Today works. Could do a two for one special and combine it with a viewing of *Casablanca* if you want to bring it over later afternoon or evening. I'll cook."

Is this a date? I'm not ready to date. Dani could feel her chest tightening and her breathing becoming more rapid.

"It's not a date. I just like to cook and evenings after chores are easier to relax and do something fun." Dani felt the air return to her lungs.

"What time and where do I need to take the picture?" She was still debating on the movie and supper, but it did sound nice. He responded that his friend was available all day and gave an address on Main in Osage. No more mention of the movie and supper offer. When her panic had subsided, Dani texted back.

"I'll plan to be there around 4:30. And supper sounds nice. What can I bring?" She smiled. She returned a missed text from Kat, but didn't tell her about her plans with Corwin. No need to excite her unnecessarily.

The day passed quickly. Dani knew she should shower before she went. The bathroom door didn't lock but still, she made sure it was shut tightly before undressing. She checked the door compulsively. When she stepped into the shower, she moved quickly, anxiety rising in her chest. Shampooing her hair was the worst. She tried to keep her eyes open. Bad things happened when her eyes were closed. But sometimes, the shampoo ran down and she had to close them for a moment. A lot could happen in a moment. She took a deep breath and stepped back into the water to rinse out the shampoo. She rinsed carefully, fingers starting at her forehead and moving back. She'd nearly finished with the water pressure stuttered and she started in surprise, sending suds down her face. She closed her eyes reflexively and felt his hot breath on her neck, his hands on her hips. She flailed toward the door, telling herself it was a memory but unable to keep herself from fleeing. Eyes still closed against the suds, Dani flung the shower door open and groped for her towel. She wiped her face and opened her eyes. She looked around, almost surprised to find herself kneeling on the bath mat in her own house instead of in the rental's cheap khaki colored bathroom with him bearing down on her. Her breath was still coming fast and shallow, and she fought to slow it down. *Five things I can see.* She counted as her eyes flitted around the room. *Four things I can touch.* She stroked the towel, bathmat, ceramic sink, and tile floor. *Three things I can hear.* Her breathing was easier now. *Two things I can smell.* She inhaled deeply and appreciated the coconut scented shampoo for the first time. *One thing I can taste.* She drew her eyebrows together and looked around the bathroom. *Water?* Dani finished her shower. Not without anxiety, but calmer than before.

Back in her room, Dani picked through her meager wardrobe. It wasn't a date, but she found herself wanting him to think she looked good anyway. She chose a soft, green v-neck t-shirt and jeans and whipped her hair up into a bun.

Dani pulled into a parking spot and double checked the address Corwin had sent her. Her heart was racing and she wished she'd asked Corwin if he was going to be here. She took a deep breath, picked up the photograph off of the passenger seat, and climbed out of the car. Her hand was on the curved brass door handle when a voice startled her.

"Goodness, you're not just punctual, you're early." His smiled faded. "Hey, I didn't mean to scare you. Are you okay?"

Dani realized her hand was curled tightly around the door handle, back pressed to the door, and she was shaking. She dropped her hand to her side. "Yes. Fine." She knew her voice was shaky. "You just. I didn't expect you."

Corwin looked unconvinced. He cocked his head, studying her. "I can't decide if you look like you've seen a ghost or if you were afraid I wasn't one."

Dani forced a smile. "You just startled me. That's all." She pulled the door open. "Shall we?"

Sarah was a short, thin woman with curly grey hair pulled into a low ponytail. She tugged on gloves before taking the photograph from Dani, who was suddenly keenly aware that she'd been touching it with her bare hands. Sarah studied the back of the photograph carefully, tipping it back and forth to vary the light.

"I can certainly let you know what this says. Did you need anything else? Would you like it restored? It's really not in bad shape." She turned the photograph over, peering intently at it. "A bit of yellowing, but I'd suggest simply placing it between acid free paper."

Dani nodded. "I can do that. For now, though, I just want to know what it says. What will we have to do to find out?"

"Nothing too extreme." She placed the photo on a scanner and clicked a few buttons on her computer. She swung the monitor around so that Dani and Corwin could see. Dani leaned forward, watching as Sarah applied filters and sharpened the image.

"Jillian?" Dani felt her breath catch in her throat.

"Maybe, let me try," Sarah's voice trailed off as she made further adjustments. Dani didn't realize she was holding her breath until Corwin tapped her on the shoulder.

"You do remember how to breathe, right?" Dani let out a burst of air and turned to him, laughing.

"I have some experience with the topic, yes."

"Aha!" Dani jumped. She hadn't expected such a loud sound from such a small woman. Sarah pointed to the screen. "Plain as day. 'Jake & Jillian, 1970' and the next line says 'Bandit,' which I'm guessing is the dog."

Dani tried to mask her disappointment. She'd hoped for a last name or a location. "Thank you so much. Could you possibly print that for me?" Sarah placed the original in an envelope before handing it and the print out to Dani. "What do I owe you?" Dani reached for her wallet, but when she looked up, Sarah was waving her away.

"No friend of Corwin pays for such an easy request. He'll just owe me dinner." She winked at Corwin and Dani raised an eyebrow. *Does everyone in town have a crush on this man?*

Corwin laughed. "Now, Sarah, you know my heart couldn't take that. Thank you, though. I'm flattered." He placed a hand on Dani's back and pushed her toward the door. "See you next time." To Dani, who was laughing hysterically, he muttered, "Hush. She'll hear you."

At Corwin's house, Dani perched on a stool at his kitchen island and watched him cook, still poking fun at him for apparently being the most eligible bachelor in town. "You said you like your steak extra peppery, right?" He held the pepper above her steak in mock threat.

"No, no, please. I'll stop. I promise." He put the pepper grinder down, but within easy reach.

"Was the writing Sarah found any help? I'd hate to think I subjected myself to her ogling for nothing."

"Well," Dani made a face. "I was really hoping for a location or a last name. But the year could be helpful. It does tell me that it wasn't taken at my house. It definitely looked basically the way it does now by 1970."

"I guess that's something." Corwin fussed over the steaks, now sizzling in a cast iron pan, and tossed some spices onto a colorful mix of vegetables in another.

Plates loaded with more food than Dani could imagine eating, they settled onto the couch with TV trays.

"Okay, brace yourself for the greatest cinematic experience of your life."

"Wow. Don't build it up or anything." Corwin smirked and hit play. A spinning globe whirred onto the screen and a voice over began giving background information. Dani groaned. "No, please tell me this whole thing is not narrated."

Corwin shushed her. "It's important. And no."

"Did they just shoot a guy? In the street? I thought this was supposed to be some great love story."

"It is. Just wait. You have to understand the time." Corwin turned to see Dani grinning at him. "Oh. You're messing with me."

"Maybe. Just a little." She smiled and turned back to the movie. "This is the best meal I've had in a long time, by the way."

Nearly two hours later, Dani found herself totally relaxed in a near food coma as the movie ended. "Hey, that's the line. And if you keep feeding me like this, then this is indeed the beginning of a beautiful friendship."

Dani dreamt of *Casablanca* that night, and spent much of the next day daydreaming about being Ingrid Bergman, faced with staying in danger for love or fleeing for wealth and stability. Like *The Woman in White*, the choices were impossible, and the heroine had much to bear either way. She'd filled Kat in on the evening, which had ended with Corwin softly snoozing on the couch while she let herself out. Kat, predictably, could not be convinced that it wasn't a date, though the fact that Corwin had fallen asleep before Dani left gave some credence to the idea that it really was just a friendship.

"I'm a little embarrassed that I fell asleep last night. It was a long day. Did you make it home okay?" Dani smiled at the text from Corwin.

"Good morning, sleeping beauty. I made it home just fine. You clearly needed the rest. No worries." Between lighthearted texts with her friends, Dani managed to restore some order to her kitchen and do some work on her classes. By the time she dropped into bed, she was exhausted and smiling, even if she did avoid the shower.

By Saturday evening, Dani was feeling brave. She even put Anika back in her pen instead of leaving her to fend for herself. Back inside, she took a quick shower with no breakdown and poured herself some whiskey. She nestled herself onto the couch and scrolled social media. Her brain needed a break, she told herself, but the truth was that her brain simply refused to be brought to bear on anything.

As she scrolled, Dani's mind wandered to her visions from J. The bedroom decor was interesting, but not exactly helpful. *But it is what I asked for.* She swirled the whiskey in her glass. *I was wishing I knew what it looked like, so . . . It's what I asked for.* Dani sat up.

"It's what I asked for." She drank the rest of her whiskey in one swig and slammed the glass down on the coffee table. "Alright, Jilly, time for some answers." Dani stood and marched upstairs and into Jilly's room.

J's window was open when Dani flipped on the light. No surprise. *What do I ask?* Dani stood in the center of the room, awaiting inspiration. *There's so much I want to know. Where to start? What can she show me here?* Already the mist was creeping in. *If I don't choose soon, she will.* Dani closed her eyes, picturing what she'd already seen here. The nightstands. That was it.

"Who slept in this room?" Dizziness overtook her and Dani sank to the floor, eyes still squeezed shut. Slowly, she opened her eyes. Jilly was sitting up in the bed, back against the headboard, the lamp next to her on, a thick book open in her lap. She stared at Dani. No. She stared through Dani, as if at something behind her. Dani turned, the dizziness making her move slowly. The hallway light was on. A man was silhouetted in the doorway. He was tall with shaggy hair, but Dani couldn't make much else out against the light.

"Come to bed, Jake." Dani's head spun to Jilly, the source of the voice. Dizziness overwhelmed her and she hunched over, bracing her hands on the floor. "Where have you been?"

Jake walked through Dani. A disconcerting concept, but Dani decided to worry about it later.

"I was just in the barn."

"Doing what? There's practically nothing left in there. "

"Oh, just hanging up some tools and leaving breadcrumbs for the birds." He'd reached the bed and flicked his lamp on. Dani could have sworn he'd looked right at her as he spoke. *Not possible. This is just Jilly's memory.* He walked back toward the door and Dani scootched out of the way, no desire to feel a memory walk through her again. *Did he just smile at me? No. Not possible.* Jake turned off the hall light and returned to the bedroom, stubbing his toe on the door jamb on his way. He cursed, hopping on one foot while he rubbed his toe. "Stupid light switch needs to be closer to the door." *I agree. Why didn't you fix that?*

"Do we really have to leave?" Jilly put a tasseled bookmark into her book and set it on her side table, then drew her knees to her chest. "I love this old house and Liam has been a great help." *Liam? Papa?*

Jake ran his hand through his shaggy black hair and sighed. "Yes, Jilly. We've been over this. I can't afford this place anymore and besides, there's too much history here. Even with Liam's help I can't change the past." *What past? What does Papa have to do with this?*

Jilly tucked her chin behind her knees and Dani recognized that comforting, defensive position. "Oh, Jilly," she whispered. Jake began unbuttoning his shirt in silence. The conversation seemed to be over, but Dani could almost feel Jilly thinking. Tiny lights flicked in the gauze of memory surrounding Dani, like that static she used to watch as she carefully peeled her blankets apart in the dark. "Don't say it." But she knew Jilly would. Knew it as if it was her own mouth that wouldn't stay obediently shut.

"What past?" Jilly lifted her chin, looking into Jake's eyes. He finished unbuttoning his shirt, never breaking eye contact, and took it off, laying it neatly on the bed. Dani thought he wasn't going to answer. He unbuckled his belt, whipped it out of his jeans, and coiled it neatly next to his shirt on the bed. Jilly flinched at this movement and broke eye contact, tucking her chin back behind her knees.

"You know damn well what past."

"You said it was an accident."

"It was, but that doesn't mean they'll ever let me forget. She died, Jilly. That's not the kind of thing they'll forgive me for." Jake was down to his boxers now, but somehow Dani found him even more intimidating mostly naked than he'd been fully dressed. He was muscular with a clear farmer's tan, even in the dim light of the dark bedroom. He picked up his belt, letting the buckle dangle toward the floor while he wrapped the other end around his hand. "And apparently it's not the kind of thing you're going to let me forget, either." He swung the buckle up to meet his free hand, shortened the belt another turn around his hand, and tried again.

Jilly kept silent, chin still tucked behind her knees. Her eyes were squeezed shut, but Dani was sure she knew exactly what Jake was doing. His movements seemed practiced, familiar. This was a game Jilly could not win in which the goal was to elicit a reaction and Jake would go as far as he needed to get one.

"The safety should have been on. I know that. But it wasn't. She's dead. They cleared me of wrongdoing. Why can't you people see that?" He was yelling now. His belt buckle thumped against his right palm faster and faster.

"It's only a memory. It's only a memory. It's only a memory." As if he could hear Dani's words, Jake turned toward her and walked to the foot of the bed, staring in her direction. Behind him, Jilly scrambled out of bed. "Jilly, no. Whatever you're doing, don't. Please. Don't." A sense of dread had joined the dizziness in the pit of Dani's stomach. Jilly crouched by the bed and glanced around the room as if trying to decide where to go. She didn't stand a chance of getting to the door with Jake at the foot of the bed. Under the bed would offer only brief protection. They were on the second story, so a window wasn't much of an option. Still, her eyes flitted about. She was determined to find a path to freedom. To safety.

"Do you have somebody else in this house?" Jake whirled back to face Jilly, only briefly thrown off by her change in location. Jilly shook her head. "I heard him. Who is he? Where is he?" Jilly shook her head again. "Answer me, woman!"

"There's no one. No one here. I don't know–" Jake walked toward her, arm raised.

"No," Dani yelled. Jake froze. He turned around, arm still raised.

"Where the fuck is he?" He turned back around. "Where, Jilly? You tell me or so help me, God, I'll beat it out of you." Jilly stood, chin high, hand clenched at her sides. She glanced at Dani and nodded, almost imperceptibly. *Can she see me?*

"There's no one here," she said firmly, even as Jake descended on her, belt still raised. She didn't flinch as the first blow landed on her shoulder, though she twisted under its weight. When Jake rose up, preparing to deliver another blow, Jilly slid to the side, away from the bed. Jake's arm was already crashing down before he realized she'd moved. Unable to stop the movement, the buckle scarred the nightstand.

"Stop it. I don't want to see this." Dani trembled. The gauzy vision, the dizziness, it was all bad enough without watching Jilly being beaten. It didn't stop. Jake had spun around and blocked Jilly's exit. He walked toward her and she backed up instinctively until her back was pressed against a window.

"Nowhere left to go, is there, Jilly? Maybe you can understand how I feel now. It's an awful feeling, isn't it?" Jilly's hands skittered across the glass for a moment, searching for anything she might be able to use. Finding nothing, she clenched her hands at her sides again and tilted her chin up. She was nothing if not strong. "Maybe now you can understand how I feel, with the cops telling me it wasn't my fault but that woman's parents blaming me. Dragging me through civil court. My own family thinking I'm nuts. I shot her because she crept up on me. That's all. I should have had the safety on until I evaluated the threat. I know that. But I didn't. It was an accident. An honest accident." He paused and Jilly realized he was desperate for assurance. Jilly kept her chin up and closed her eyes.

"Actually, there is somewhere you can go." Jake leaned forward, placing his hands on either side of Jilly, letting the belt buckle smack against the window pane. Suddenly, he pushed upward and the window was open. Jilly gasped in unison with Dani. There was no screen on the window. Probably not on any of the windows. "Sit down."

"What?" Jilly was momentarily stunned out of silence.

"You heard me. Sit. Down." Jilly clenched her jaw. Seeing that she wasn't moving to sit down, Jake pushed down on her shoulders, forcing her to the windowsill. Her head just cleared the sash and she clutched the windowsill to steady herself. Her hair blew forward on a breeze that cooled the room. Dani crawled closer to the window. "Now you stay there and we'll see just how many hits you can take. I bet you're not so brave this time." Jilly raised her chin in defiance as Jake raised the belt. The first blow crashed into her ribs and she wobbled backward, knuckles white against the windowsill. She steadied herself. The next blow struck her breast and she screamed, stomach tightening to keep herself upright. "You're a stubborn little bitch." Jake gritted his teeth and swung again. This time, the buckle caught Jilly square in the eye. A strangled screech and then she was falling.

Dani ran to the window, ignoring the feeling of the memory passing through her as Jake, too, looked down. Jilly lay in the flowerbed below. Still. *It's only two stories. Surely she's not gone yet.* She watched for any sign of movement, knowing she couldn't help either way. Jake ran to Jilly's side, yelling her name, as if he wasn't the one who'd just knocked her out the window. Jilly turned her head, eyes still closed, and Dani breathed an irrational sigh of relief. Jake's voice turned from concern to anger.

"You survived that? I guess you needed a longer fall." He looked around, as if one might open up next to him at any moment. "Or a harder landing." He reached for something hidden from Dani's view by the brushy flowers. When he placed it next to Jilly's head, Dani could see that it was a pale rock. The kind available in spades around here and that still bordered the flowerbeds. Jake cradled Jilly's head in his hands and leaned close to her. For a moment, Dani thought he might kiss her, but then he lifted her head even higher and slammed it onto the rock.

Dani screamed. She couldn't watch. She sat back onto the floor and stared out the window, praying the memory would end. She didn't want to watch, or hear, any more of this. A flicker of light caught her eye. It was in the shed across the driveway from the house. She shook her head. Probably nothing. But there it was again. Someone was out there. Someone who might be able to see what was happening in the dim lights from the porch and bedroom. Someone who, based on the height of the flashlight, couldn't be more than a teenager.

~ 9 ~

A faint but persistent dinging roused Dani. She peeled her head from the pillow, appalled to find drool wetting the fabric. Her head felt like cotton and she was certain her breath was repulsive. *What on earth is wrong with me?* She rifled through her sheets, finally landing a hand on her phone. The dinging was louder, freed from the muffling effect of the sheets.

"Shut up." She pressed the home button to end the sound, but not before seeing the label she'd attached to the alarm: Church. "Ugh." Dani flopped back, but sprang back up immediately on touching the cold wet corner of her pillow. "Fine. But I'm not showering first." She eyed the whiskey bottle on the floor, considering the hair of the dog treatment, but opted instead for the bottle of water on her dresser. She pulled on her chore clothes, noting that they were a bit looser than they'd been, and stepped into the hall. *What the . . .* Plaster dust was blown from the room at the other end of the hall all the way to her bedroom door. It stopped in a neat line at the threshold. Jilly's bedroom door was wide open. In a rush, Dani remembered what she'd drunk so much to forget last night. The vicious beating. The murder. The watcher in the barn.

Dani's phone pinged. Her mother. "Are you riding with us again this week?" Dani shook her head to clear it. She responded as she ran down the stairs. She'd have to hurry, but today, she didn't feel like driving. The calves were skittish this morning, but they were all there. The boars chuffed at her as she tossed them food and splashed water into their pans. Anika was out, as usual, but went in on seeing Dani. Aside from the pounding of her head, it was a pretty easy chore morning.

Back inside, Dani flicked the coffee pot on and went upstairs to find something approximating "dressy" for church. Could she rock heels and pearls? Absolutely. Was she going to today? No way in hell. Or heaven. She selected dark jeans and a purple mock-silk top. She hadn't bothered to rescue much in the way of accessories, so her standard silver dove necklace would have to do. Satisfied that she at least looked like she hadn't just rolled out of bed, Dani brushed her teeth, filled a travel mug with coffee, and headed up to Mom's.

Dani tried to ignore glares from the elderly church-goers as she made her way to their pew. Her coffee wasn't gone and she dang sure needed it today, so this cup was coming with her. Her jeans probably weren't helping, either. *Whatever. Y'all are lucky this is just coffee.* She smiled and nodded at her parents' friends, who seemed more accepting of her. Finally, she slid into the pew and crossed her legs, relaxing into a sip of coffee.

"Oh my gosh. I haven't stopped thinking about you." The voice in Dani's ear startled her, and she found herself gagging on coffee. Someone patted her on the back as she tried to regain her breath. Coffee finally cleared from her airways, Dani turned to see who had interrupted her peace. Marie. Of course. She restrained herself from rolling her eyes.

"Hi, Marie. You startled me."

"I could see that. I am so sorry. I did not mean to. I totally thought you saw me there. It's such a small church. I can't believe you missed me. Maybe you didn't. But you definitely missed me sliding into the pew to talk to you, now didn't you? Anyway, I haven't been able to stop thinking about you. That house is just so incredible and I'm so happy that you're fixing it up. How's that going? Do you need help? I hope I didn't scare you with that ghost thing. It's totally not a ghost. That's just what my dad thought for a little bit. People get weird ideas. You understand? Oh, and I remembered. We found this picture. It was old, with the curvy edges. Do you know what I mean? Like the picture was black and white but there was this white curvy edge around it, too? It has to be from like the 1800s or something. It had these people and a dog and a house. We put it back where it fell from. One of the windows, if I remember right. We thought it would freak Dad out, so we didn't want him to see."

Dani shifted in her seat, taking a careful sip of coffee. Marie was more than a little off in her estimate of the photo's age, but still, it was definitely the same one. So the picture had been there all along, too.

"It was a cool picture, though. I always wanted a dog, so I used to imagine that one running around the house. Dad would have never allowed a dog. He said he was allergic but I think he just didn't want another mouth to feed. Now that I'm an adult, I can't say I blame him. I get it. But gosh, it would have been fun–"

"Good morning!" The elder leading the service called everyone to order. Dani couldn't remember his name, but she was extremely thankful for him. Marie sat back, apparently willing to abide by church rules. Dani made sure to excuse herself to go to the bathroom during the greeting time, so as to avoid conversation with Marie at least until the end of the service.

As she squeezed past her parents into the pew, Mother whispered "You'd be able to say good morning to people if you'd leave your coffee in the car."

"Precisely," she mumbled.

"What?" Mother whispered back. Dani shook her head, mouthed "Nothing" and plopped down, feigning interest in the bulletin.

Once she felt her mother's eyes shift back to the front of the church and off of her, Dani grabbed a pencil from the holder on the pew and flipped to the blank space on the back of the bulletin. She drew a line down the center and labeled the left side "Letter" and the right side "Memory." Vivid as the vision had been, Dani felt certain it had to be real. But then it didn't match the letter explaining what had happened. So, she did what she did best: made a list. Under the "Letter" heading, she listed the basics: Jilly shot, Jake PTSD,

Jake nightmare, Jake in Vietnam, Jake ran away. Across from them, she listed the coordinating facts from the memory: Jilly beaten, Jake past accident, Jake abusive, No Vietnam ref - PTSD?, Watcher in the barn. She studied the lists for a moment. Aside from the possibility of PTSD and Jake running away, neither of which was certain, there was no overlap. *Why doesn't your letter match what happened, Jake?*

Dani flipped the bulletin over to conceal the lists and stared blankly at the pastor. After a few opening comments reminding the congregation that he was preaching through the gospel of Matthew and that, at this point, Jesus was in the height of his ministry following John the Baptist's death, he asked everyone to open their Bibles to Matthew 15. Dani made no move to comply. Her Bible had been left behind anyway, when she left him, and besides, she knew this section well enough. She couldn't wait to hear how this pastor handled Jesus comparing the Canaanite woman, or her people, really, with dogs.

"Chapter fifteen begins with Jesus and his disciples breaking tradition and redefining their importance. If you've been with us through Matthew so far, you'll remember that Jesus's actions and parables go against the Pharisee's traditions and laws. They don't fast, they speak and associate with foreign women, and they certainly don't show the same fear of the unclean that the Pharisees do. They are acting out radical love and dismantling the Pharisees' teachings and traditions one by one. Rest assured, the actual laws of God stay in place. Jesus isn't condoning murder or adultery here. But in 15:5-6, we get a glimpse into how the Pharisees were intentionally avoiding following the law. Jesus says 'But you say, "If anyone tells his father or his mother, 'What you would have gained from me is given to God,' he need not honor his father."' Essentially, the Pharisees were teaching that if you give your money to the temple, you are no longer required to financially care for your aging parents.

It's easy to slip into thinking that the Pharisees surely meant well. And some probably did. But this passage makes it clear that their intentions were overtly evil, removing support even from the elderly and widowed in order to get money for themselves through the temple. Later, in 15:14, Jesus refers to the Pharisees as 'blind guides' and states that 'if the blind lead the blind, both will fall into a pit.' Since the Pharisees carefully kept the law and the traditions surrounding the law, this statement would have been shocking. But Jesus emphasizes that it doesn't matter how well they keep Kosher or wash as prescribed, their words, thoughts, and false teachings make them unclean."

Dani nodded. So far, so good. She tuned out as he went into more detail about the Levitical laws and Pharisees. She flipped back to the lists on the back of the bulletin. She felt on the verge of realizing something when her phone buzzed. Glancing at her mother and finding her focused on the pastor, Dani risked a glance down.

"It's been awhile. Do you miss me yet?" Dani uncrossed her legs and sat ramrod straight, feeling the color drain from her face.

"This next section, 15:21-28, can be a bit tough. Stay with me here, because Jesus isn't being as harsh as you might initially think." Dani swallowed and stared hard at the pastor. "We see a Canaanite woman asking Jesus for the healing of her daughter. His initial response is that he was sent to Israel, the Jews, and that it isn't right to give the children's food to the dogs. In this image, the children are the Jews and the dogs are the Canaanites. But he's not calling her a dog. We need to remember that this is the man who just dismantled the Levitical laws on cleanliness. He's not necessarily interested in keeping or drawing divisions between people."

Dani's phone vibrated against her hand on the pew. "Really? No response? I know you saw it. Jesus had it right. Women = Dogs." Dani flipped the phone over, feeling her heart race and the air leave her lungs. She fought for breath and stared back at the pastor, refusing to give him the pleasure of seeing her look for him.

"—doesn't argue with him. She just says 'Okay, maybe I'm a dog, but even dogs get crumbs.' Jesus rewards her for her faith, for her belief that he had enough power left over to heal her daughter even after ministering to all of Israel. And here's the important thing about this interaction: He healed her daughter instantly. He didn't make the woman prove her faith any further. He didn't question her daughter's faith. He didn't make her convert to Judaism. Even though he uses the Pharisees' point of view to describe the Canaanites as dogs under a dinner table, he then breaks that division down by, metaphorically, feeding the children's food directly to the dogs, making them children as well. Our Savior values women, outcasts, and gentiles. Praise the Lord for that."

Another vibration. Dani forced herself not to look. It would just be him. Or if not he'd think she was checking his messages again. *Where are you?* Still, she wouldn't look around. He was here. Okay. But now *she* would dictate how this went down. *I can count on Marie for some after church conversation, bless her heart.* Dani went through the motions of the remainder of the service. Standing to sing when it was time, and mouthing the words to keep from being glared at by her mother. Finally, Pastor gave the benediction. Dani shoved her phone in her pocket without looking at it, hoping that if he could see her, he'd get the hint that she was in no mood for him and his bullshit. Not that it had ever stopped him before.

Dani turned to follow her parents out of the pew and Marie walked next to her, one pew over, chattering about the sermon. Dani nodded automatically, hoping her grunts of acknowledgment matched whatever Marie was saying. She kept her eyes fixed on the back of her father's boots in front of her. They were stopped in the aisle now, her father's baritone voice asking after someone's health. She watched other shoes shuffle past them, the occasional greeting floating in the air as they left her vision. Pink, pointed toe loafers entered her vision, but these stopped in front of her, and Dani knew she'd have to look up eventually. Then, a pair of brown leather boots with rounded toes, the kind some men wear to hike in but that he'd always used as dress shoes appeared next to the pink loafers. Dani couldn't breathe.

"Look who I found hiding in the back of the church," Judy was excited. She had no idea what she'd just brought on Dani.

"He said your phone must not be working so he wasn't sure where you were and I said, 'Well, honey, they're sittin' where they always sit. I'll show ya.' So here he is, doll. You two are just precious together." Dani's eyes trailed up Judy's slim form in her neatly pressed pantsuit. She was beaming, clearly excited to reunite the happy couple. He smirked over her shoulder, towering above them both. Her father had fallen silent. He might not know why his baby girl was back home, but he knew dang well this wasn't right, and Dani could sense it in the hand he placed on her shoulder. *Fuck it.*

"We're divorced, Judy. I'm so sorry you had to find out this way. He's been stalking me, so I can promise you he knew exactly where I was. He's sat in this pew with us before. He just thought I wouldn't tell you what was going on. It's a game he likes to play. I'm so sorry he involved you." Dani felt her jaw drop and snapped it shut. *Where did that come from?* She knew she'd said it, of course, but how? Why? Where had the strength come from? Over his shoulder, a firefly-fast light flickered. "Thanks, Jilly," she whispered. Her father's head snapped in her direction and she wondered briefly if it was because his little angel had just dared to tell off her ex husband or because he'd heard her utter Jilly's name.

He stood in shocked silence for only a moment. "Now that's not quite true, is it, honey? I signed your divorce papers so you could have your little boyfriend, but I said we'd still date. And then you were gone. I was worried about you. I thought maybe he'd kidnapped you. I had to look after you." He smiled and Dani wanted to hurl. Judy had turned the color of her frilly white shirt and mumbled something unintelligible as she backed away. Papa's fingers clenched her shoulder tighter.

"Not the time. Not the place." He pulled Dani closer. "The papers are signed. It's over. Don't come back." Dani knew there would be questions later, but in this moment, she was grateful for her father's strong grip as he pulled her out of the church. Once they were out on the sidewalk, he released Dani, but he didn't stop until they reached the car.

Her mother peppered them with questions that neither of them bothered to answer. "You didn't know he was coming? Where has he been? Why didn't he just come sit with us if he wanted to see you so bad? Liam, did you hear what he said about a boyfriend? Do you have a boyfriend, Dani? Why did you leave him, anyway? He's a looker." They got in the car and Dani finally felt she could breathe. "Why is no one answering me? Answer me."

Liam turned to his wife. "It's okay, dear. Dani will fill us in over lunch. Just relax." The ride home was silent. Dani turned over the options in her head. She could tell them only what they basically already knew after the confrontation. That would be enough to satisfy them, and she knew they wouldn't push. On the other hand, if he turned up again, he could reveal more and then they'd think she was lying. How much did a parent really want to know about their child's marriage?

Sandwiches made and chips distributed, Dani settled in to eat, praying her parents would be too nervous about the answers to ask their questions. Her father let her get a few bites in before clearing his throat.

"Let's hear it." Mouth full, Dani nodded. But she chewed and swallowed as slowly as she could, mind and heart racing.

"He wasn't good. To me. When he was sober, he was what you saw today. Manipulative, but not overly dangerous." She stared at her plate. "When he was drinking, he hurt me. At first, he'd apologize the next day. Then it became my fault. I provoked him. I spent too much money. I didn't have supper ready." *Too much detail. They don't need to know everything.* "Anyway, that's why I left."

The table was silent. Dani took a bite of her sandwich, but her parents weren't eating. They were staring at her. She didn't want to know what they were thinking. Finally, her mother broke the silence.

"And the boyfriend?"

"There wasn't one. Isn't one. He started drinking one day and I knew I couldn't take it so I made up some excuse and left. I went to Kat's and I didn't come back. He's been convinced I was at a boyfriend's house ever since."

Her father cleared his throat and looked down at his hands on the table. "Why didn't you call me?"

"Oh, Papa." Dani felt her chest tighten as tears slid down her cheeks. "I didn't want to involve anybody else. I didn't know what he'd do. But I knew where I could come when I left." She put her hand on his. "I couldn't have left without you." He met her gaze. His eyes, usually a pale blue, were a steely grey.

"I'm glad you came home." He pushed his unfinished lunch away. "Why don't we go work on that old house of yours today?"

With her parents' help, it didn't take long to sweep the plaster in Jilly's room into neat piles near the windows under which the dumpster would be placed the next day. They finished gutting the upstairs bath, which included knocking down some plaster, and removed the tattered carpet from the room across from hers before breaking for a snack. Sweaty and filthy, they sat on the empty dining room floor eating Oreos and chugging water. Dani had considered sneaking whiskey into her cup, but there'd be hell to pay if her mother caught her.

"You really haven't made any effort to make this place home, Dani. When are you going to do that?"

Dani bit back a number of sarcastic replies about stalking, haunting, and a lack of funds. "Maybe I'll go get a few things today," she said instead. No sense in breaking their tenuous peace. "I know I want to make that big room into my bedroom."

Her father frowned. "There's no closet in there."

"So? It's gutted anyway. I can build a closet in before I hang the new sheetrock. I love how many windows it has. And it's nice and cool, even in the summer." She watched his face for any reaction.

Liam grunted. "I guess. But it'll be drafty. And lots of light on those summer nights when you're trying to sleep."

"So I'll save up for new windows and hang curtains." He was edging closer to saying what he meant, she was sure of it.

"People say it's," he paused, as if uncertain of the next word, "haunted. I don't believe in such things, but I know you do. Thought it might matter."

"Haunted? By who?" No sense in letting him know that Marie had told her exactly that information already. Might as well see how much he'd be willing to admit.

"I'm sure I have no idea. It's just what people say." Dani thought for a moment. *How can I keep him talking?*

"Oh, wait. I found something I wanted to show you." She raced upstairs and grabbed the photograph of the couple with the dog. If he wouldn't tell her on his own, maybe physical evidence would open his lips. "This was under one of the windowsills. Any idea who it is? They must have at least lived here, or their relatives did." She handed the photograph over to her father.

He held the photograph with both hands, thumbs and forefingers gently pinching the scalloped white edge. The muscles in his jaw worked, as if clenching and unclenching his teeth. Her mother leaned over to peek at the photograph, apparently wondering what had Liam so focused and silent.

"Is that Bandit?" She pointed to the dog. "It kind of looks like Bandit from those photo albums your mom did." He looked up, then, but he didn't see them. He was somewhere else. Some time else.

"Yes. That's Bandit. He was a great dog. Took good care of his sheep." Liam frowned down at the picture. "You're wondering who they are."

"I don't remember seeing them in your photo albums," Mother pried the picture from his hands and examined it closer. "He kind of looks like you, in the nose. Maybe the eyes, too. It's hard to tell from this picture. A cousin or something?"

Liam took a deep breath, palms on his thighs as if to steady himself. "A brother."

No one moved. Dani could swear no one breathed. Not even a dust mote dared shift in the sunlight. Then, a thump from upstairs. Liam looked up. "And Jilly."

Liam was, traditionally, a man of few words. He always had been. As a baby, his mother had worried that he'd never talk, only to discover that he was perfectly well spoken when he needed to be. She claimed his first word had actually been a complete sentence. Dani had doubted this story. Until today. Even after identifying the people in the photograph, Liam's story did not spill out. Getting him to talk was something more akin to a pry bar and rusty nails.

"If that's Jilly, then is that Jake? That's not this house, is it?" Dani frowned, trying again to make the house in the photo make sense.

"How did you know that?"

"What?"

"His name."

"Oh. Um." *Shit. Truth or hide?* "I saw his name on something." She could see from her father's face that she'd have to tell him more. "There was a letter hidden in the barn. It was from him."

"You went in that falling down old barn?" *Yes, way to stay on task, Mama.*

"What did it say?" Papa's face was grim. Dani got the distinct feeling that he thought he knew.

"Let me get it." She retrieved the letter and sat studying her father's face as he read it. She knew he was a fast reader.

That's where she got it from. But he studied that letter at least twice as long as it should have taken him to read it. Finally, he folded it and slid it back into the tattered envelope.

"He was in Vietnam. That's true. He was haunted after." When it was clear that he wasn't going to say any more on the subject without prompting, Dani cleared her throat.

"Did he really do that? To Jilly, I mean?" She felt like a liar, asking her father a question she knew the answer to. One he was likely to lie about because he couldn't possibly know that she knew. Maybe he didn't even know it wasn't true. He wouldn't have been very old at the time. A preteen, or maybe an early teenager. Dani didn't bother to do the exact math.

Liam took a deep breath. "He killed her, yes." *Way to dodge that question, Papa.* "And then he disappeared." Dani scrunched her eyebrows. He was avoiding details. Was he being his usual taciturn self or was he hiding something? "Did you find anything else?"

"No. Should I have?" *Two can play at this game, Papa.* She hoped her face looked the picture of innocence. *I just wish I was better at poker.*

Liam was unwilling to reveal more, and eventually they resumed work. Next up was assessing the condition of the plaster in the middle bedroom upstairs. Dani said a silent prayer that it was in good condition so she could at least put off destroying and re-sheetrocking another room. First they needed to move the wall of boxes so that they could see clearly what they were working with. The three formed a mini chain to pass boxes from the room out into the hallway, where they were stacked one deep and three high, leaving room for Dani to navigate. According to the neatly written labels, the dust coated boxes contained mostly children's toys. As old as they were, they were likely worth something.

"Is this stuff we need to go through and keep some, or can it just go away?" Dani heaved a box labeled "train set" to the floor. "I bet some of it is worth something by now."

Liam grunted as he hoisted a box down from the top of a precarious tower to pass to Mama. "Oh, I suppose some of it might be, but mostly it's junk." He glanced at the label on the box he was holding. "Teddy bears from an abandoned house probably won't be in great shape anyway." Dani looked to the edges of the room. There was some evidence of rodent activity, but she hadn't seen chew marks on any boxes so far. Just dust. Lots and lots of dust.

"But you're good if I go through and get rid of it? Do we even know whose it was?"

"Jilly's. And Jake's." He passed another box to Mama, who shifted it onto Dani's waiting arms.

"They had kids?" Jilly hadn't shown her any kids.

"No. Jilly wanted them, so she kept toys from their childhoods. Bought toys at sales. She dreamed."

"What about the people who lived here after them? Why didn't they get it out of their way?"

"This room was always locked when Dad rented the place. It was never part of the deal. Not after Jilly."

They worked in silence after that, finally clearing enough boxes to give a clear view of the walls. A telltale dark stain on the ceiling and buckling at the top of one wall told Dani exactly what she didn't want to know: this plaster had to come down, too.

"Ugh. Another gut job. These boxes have to go somewhere so I can do that, Papa. So can I go through them?" The silence stretched on so long that Dani considered repeating herself. Papa was getting a little hard of hearing, thanks to spending the bulk of his life on a tractor.

"I don't see–" Mama's voice was hesitant and her eyes fixed on Papa as she spoke.

"You can go through them. But bring anything you decide to get rid of to me first."

"Okay. I think it's time for supper. You want to come up after you clean up a little?" Mama's voice was just a little too bright.

"Sure, Mama. Maybe tomorrow you can go to the city with me to get some supplies to fix up the bathroom?" Dani wished she hadn't said it. Her bank account would hate her for it, but pay day was coming and what little Mama might know could be helpful.

"Of course. I'd love to." She pecked Dani on the cheek and she and Papa headed down the stairs.

"Remember. Bring me anything you're getting rid of."

Dani leaned against the wall at the top of the stairs and watched them go. By the time the two of them got cleaned up in their one tiny bathroom, she figured she had about thirty minutes to get cleaned up herself. That left plenty of time to go through at least one box. Two if she was quick. She chose boxes still inside the room so as to speed progress toward her goal of clearing it for demolition. The first box was quick. It held a rag doll that had seen better days, Jilly's, if she had to guess, and three other baby dolls with their various clothing and bottles. *Nothing here to save*, but she set the rag doll in her room. The second box was more interesting. The label read "Trucks & Farm." Inside, Dani found die-cast tractors, trucks, and small metal animals. The paint was worn from many, and one lamb was missing a leg while a horse was short an ear, but they were incredible. A hardboard barn with a tin roof was nestled beneath packing paper in the bottom of the box. It was well-used, but in reasonably good shape. This whole set would be worth something, but Dani knew it wasn't leaving her house. She resisted the urge to erect the tiny metal fences around cows, horses, and sheep, instead returning everything to the box and placing it in the hallway near her bedroom.

Realizing she'd completely lost track of time, Dani reached to her pocket for her phone to see just how late she was going to be. It wasn't there. *Does he have it? How could he? I had it after that, right?* She patted each of her pockets in succession while she roamed the upstairs, checking every possible surface. Not in the bathroom or her bedroom. Any other surface had been moved or had things stacked on it, so there was no telling. *Downstairs, then. If he has it and he sees my conversation with Kat,* she wouldn't let herself finish the thought. She lost her footing on the landing and skidded down the final six stairs on her backside. It was getting dark downstairs, where most of the windows were east-facing, but Dani saw what little light remained reflected on the dark, shiny surface of her phone screen. She scrambled to the phone on all fours. The screen woke as she lifted it from the floor. It was filled with notifications from him. She stared at them for a moment before bursting into hysterical laughter. *He's so close, but so, so far. He could find my parents, but not me. That stupid city slicker is going to get lost and die of starvation in the country before he'd ever think to check this old, falling down, haunted house.* All the stress, frustration, fear, all of it came pouring out as she laughed until she cried. A thud sounded from upstairs. "Right, Jilly?" she choked out between breaths, "The things we let men do to us."

Only when her phone buzzed and Dani read the text from her mother asking where she was did she finally catch her breath. Wiping her eyes, she rose from the floor and hobbled to the downstairs bathroom for a quick shower, vowing to close her eyes for once. On her way, she typed, "Goodbye" without bothering to read the messages, then blocked his number.

The next morning, Dani was out of bed before her alarm went off. There was still demolition to do, but first, she and Mama were headed to the city to purchase the first pieces she'd need to put it all back together. She gave the curious calf a nose scratch with his breakfast and he bucked away from her playfully. Her other chores complete, Dani changed and drove up to Mama's. Over banana bread, they made a list of the essentials: drywall, nails, screws, mud, tape, shower surround, caulk. The list ran on and Dani's head was spinning at the potential expense. *We'll just have to prioritize.*

"Any more text messages?" Mama asked as Dani filled her travel mug with Papa's coffee. Dani smiled down at the oil slick reflection before pressing the lid on and turning back to Mama.

"No. I finally grew a pair and blocked him last night."

"Good." Mama grabbed her own shopping list and stuffed it into her purse, then pawed through it, looking for something. "What does he drive?" She didn't look up when she asked.

"Your glasses are on your head. Last I knew, a red four door something or other. Why?"

Mama patted her head. "Oh, there they are. No reason." She paused. "Just a car that looked like your old one turned around in the driveway last night. I wondered if maybe he had a matching one."

Dani felt like a deer caught in headlights. Unable to move yet sensing impending doom.

"I'm sure it's nothing. Can we take your truck? Dad needs his today." Dani was aware of following her mother to the door. Of climbing into her nice, safe, farmboy truck. Of starting that truck and driving to Menards. Of her mother telling her about her cousin's latest drama. But all she saw were headlights. And all she heard was *Run.*

Gradually, as must happen to deer caught in the headlights who survive, Dani came back to herself. Her cart was loaded with buckets of drywall screws and tubes of caulk when she heard herself telling her mother that she wanted to focus on the bathroom first. It was true, she realized, but she didn't remember the conversation leading up to this point. *Time to refocus.* She examined bathtub surrounds, debating the merits of built-in shelving with her mother. Her favorite option's price tag was more than a little shocking, but with Mama's help she found a more affordable version and they muscled the box onto the flat cart. An hour and one painful price tag later, Dani's truck was loaded up with supplies.

"You'll have to pick paint colors next. And decide what you're going to do with those old floors." Dani groaned. "You can probably restore the wood floors in some of those rooms."

"One step at a time. Please, Mama. My bank account doesn't want to think about paint and flooring right now."

Dani's phone buzzed somewhere amidst the sacks on the bench seat. She reached for it, but Mama found it first.

"You do not text and drive, young lady. Who's Corwin? And why is he offering to come help with your house?"

Dani snatched the phone away. "And you do not read other people's text messages. He's a friend of Kat's and he fixed up his own old house, so he knows a thing or two about it." She tapped out a response while her mother glared. "I asked him to come this afternoon to help clear out the debris. You can meet him then if you're so inclined." Her mother hmphed and said nothing, but Dani would have bet her last whiskey that she'd be there.

By the time they arrived back home, Dani's phone must have buzzed a half a dozen more times, but she didn't dare pick it back up. She'd already tested her mother's patience by texting and driving once. One message was from Corwin, confirming that he'd be there this afternoon. The rest were from Kat. Corwin had told her that he'd be coming over to help and Kat was full of questions and advice. Dani wasn't sure exactly how Kat thought she could manage to look cute and be ready to work at the same time, but apparently there would be a video call after lunch to help.

After a quick early lunch, Dani began unloading supplies from her pickup. She'd leave the sheetrock in the bed for the moment. Corwin could help her carry it in and lean it against the dining room wall later. She'd worked up a sweat by the time Kat called.

"No. Absolutely not."

"What?" Dani pushed frizzy hair off of her sweaty forehead.

"Bandanna. Now."

"This may come as a shock to you, but I don't care how I look. At all. He's coming to help me work. And besides, I didn't grab a lot of accessories when I left."

"At least tell me your shirt doesn't have any holes in it." Dani looked down and twisted around to examine the shirt.

"Just one on the hem." She showed Kat, who groaned. "What? At least it doesn't show anything. I could have worn the one with a rip across the chest."

"You still have that?"

"Theoretically. Not sure if it made it into my bag or not."

"Do not go find out. Just. Do you at least have a headband? Any way to tame the frizz at all?"

"No. It's fine. It's like a halo," she said, turning to back light herself in a window.

"You are hopeless. I can't work like this." There was a smile under Kat's complaints. She sighed dramatically. "You most certainly do not have a halo. Can you at least promise to be nice to him?"

"If he's nice to me," Dani laughed. "Look, I have on a shirt without obvious holes, jeans that don't give me a muffin top, and I've promised to probably be nice. What more could you want?"

"So, so much more," Kat groaned. "But I'll take what I can get."

Dani was hauling the last of the bags in from the cab of the truck when Corwin pulled in. *Early. Nice.* She nodded to him and continued inside. The bags were too heavy to worry much about politeness.

"Knock, knock," Corwin called. He sounded like he was leaning in the back door, waiting on permission to step in.

"Come on in, but we're going back out to grab the sheetrock." She heard his boots on the tile floor. He paused, debating which way to turn. Either way would work, not that he knew that. Left would talk him the slightly longer route. Right would bring him directly into the kitchen and into her eyesight. She dropped the bags to the floor a little louder than necessary, curious to see if he would pick up on it. He did.

"Kind of a maze, huh?"

"Not bad once you know it. Mind giving me a hand with the sheetrock? We'll lean it against the wall here." He nodded, but neither of them moved. Corwin was looking around the room. Although he was clearly interested in exploring, Dani took his stillness as a sign of respect for her. "I promise

I'll give you the tour after we get the sheetrock in." *Is he blushing?*

"Sorry, I've got a thing for old houses. Let's get the worst job done first, though. You're right." The two fell into a rhythm. Occasionally, they would pause for a breather after leaning their latest load against the wall. Corwin used the chance to quiz her about the house. "Do you know when this was built?"

"Not exactly. Mom and Papa's was built in 1901 and from what I understand this was built not long after."

"Redone in the 70s, I gather." He gestured to the dingy gold and green patterned wallpaper lining the dining room walls.

"Those poor people." Dani gave an exaggerated shudder. "Can you imagine being convinced that avocado green was the way to go?" Corwin laughed and they headed out for another sheet, exchanging horrible design trend barbs.

"Lace curtains."

"Yes! What's the point? Wood paneling."

"Okay, now that can be tastefully done. Orange shag carpeting."

Dani laughed as she backed up the steps with her end of the sheetrock. "You win."

Sheetrock all safely inside, Dani gave the promised tour of the house. Corwin was quiet, mostly. Occasionally he asked questions she didn't know the answer to, like if this was the original trim and whether the porch had been original or built on later. He seemed to be satisfied to simply soak in the atmosphere of the place. Upstairs, he whistled at the amount of work left to do.

"I know. We were supposed to be throwing plaster down into the dumpster today, but they had to postpone placement until tomorrow. So you get to help me sort through boxes and clear this room instead."

Corwin shoved his hands into his front jeans pockets. "You mean I get to play in old dusty vintage stuff? Sounds like one heck of a good time to me." Dani couldn't decide if he was being serious or sarcastic. Finally, he cracked a smile. "For real. I've got a collection of old cast iron cars. I love this stuff."

"Good. Some of it I'll be looking to offload, so you just name your price." They each grabbed a box and knelt to examine the contents. Trash would go into Jilly's room for easy disposal the next day. Things to keep would get stacked at the end of the hall near Dani's bedroom. Things to show her father before selling or donating would stack near the top of the stairs, preferably in condensed boxes.

Boxes of baby clothes went immediately to the top of the stairs. Dani marveled again that they hadn't been bothered by rodents. Corwin just shrugged. "With no people in and out of this room, there probably wasn't much in the way of temptation. No food, no people smells." Dani nodded, but she had a sneaking suspicion that Jilly had a lot more to do with it than that. A jack-in-the-box, blocks, and two large boxes stuffed with vintage board games joined the ever-growing pile at the top of the stairs. A box of children's books found a home near Dani's bedroom. Nothing thus far had gone to

Jilly's room for disposal. Although she didn't see much sense in keeping it, most of the things were in decent enough shape for her father to make the final call.

Corwin held up a paper doll set. "This has got to be worth something," he marveled. Many of the dolls weren't punched out, and those that were remained in pristine condition. "You should definitely get these appraised."

"You don't want to keep them to play with?" Corwin laughed and held a dress in front of one of the dolls.

"How's this look? Does it match my eyes?" His voice was high and squeaky. "I was thinking the black heels. What do you think?" A loud thump sounded from Jilly's room. Dani jumped. "What on earth was that?"

"Oh," Dani studied his face. *In for a penny, in for a pound.* "Jilly."

"And who is Jilly? I've been on the tour, so I know you don't have a roommate."

Dani took a deep breath. "I'll tell you. But I'm gonna need you to promise that you won't call the men in the little white coats." She told the story in a rush, half afraid Corwin would run when she finished.

Corwin twisted a wooden articulated snake idly in his hands. "So Jilly was murdered under her bedroom window. Why would she want to stick around?"

"Maybe she doesn't have a choice. Or she needed someone to know what really happened. Papa said Jake killed her, but I'm not sure how much anybody back then knew about what was going on here."

"It was the 70s. Not exactly a time when you'd tell the world you were on antidepressants and being beaten by your husband. I doubt anybody would have cared or done anything about it."

"Touché."

"So what happened to Jake?"

"Good question. I have a theory, but–"

"No little men in little white coats. I promise."

Dani laughed. "Okay. Papa said he disappeared. And Jake's note said he was running away, not that his note was exactly accurate."

"Where do you think he went?"

"Nowhere. I don't think he ever left."

Corwin tilted his head, brows drawn together. "Why would he stick around after something like that? Even in the 70s they would have known Jilly's death was no accident."

"Remember the person I saw watching the whole thing? What if that person didn't let him leave? What if Jake died here, too?"

"And how did they not get caught?"

"Well, it was a farm. In the 70s. There's lots of land and not a lot of nosy neighbors."

Corwin nodded, looking out a window as if trying to see Jake's body. "True enough, but I still think someone would have missed him. His family, at least."

"My family," Dani reminded him.

"Right. But you've never heard of him?"

"No. Papa just admitted to having a brother yesterday. He didn't even tell me his name. I learned that from the letter. I never knew any of them, but I'd venture a guess they weren't a super tight family. And Grandpa was gone by then anyway."

"Gone? What about Grandma?"

Dani nodded. "He died shortly after Papa was born. Grandma died when I was young. No other siblings that I know of. No cousins. I just assumed it was a tiny family."

"Maybe it is. Or maybe he cut himself off from them for some reason." They cleared several more boxes in silence before Corwin sat up, stretching his back. "I think I need a break."

"Oh. Yeah, I could probably use one, too," Dani said, pushing aside a box of photo albums that she knew her papa would need to see. "You want some water or something?" They clomped down the stairs, too tired to bother with grace. When Dani reached the bottom, she turned to ask Corwin what he wanted to drink. He was carrying two boxes. "Corwin, you didn't need to do that right now."

Corwin shrugged. "I figured they'd be going in your truck eventually and I was coming down anyway." *Whoa.*

"I. Well. Thank you."

"Sure thing. I'll toss these in the truck." Dani nodded dumbly. She got them both glasses of water, but waited to chug hers until he was back inside. They each downed two glasses while leaning against the kitchen counter, exhausted. "I should probably get home soon so I can chore." Dani felt an unexpected pang of sadness at this. "Or my parents could do them. There's not much. We could get a few more boxes cleared."

Dani groaned. "I don't think I can face any more dusty boxes right now. Besides, I don't want to keep you from whatever you need to do." Corwin laughed. *So easy.* "It has been fun, though. I haven't made many friends back here yet."

"I get it. Tackling a project this big alone would be a little daunting. I'm glad I could help." They stood in awkward silence, neither wanting to end the conversation, neither knowing how to continue. A heavy thump from upstairs made Dani jump, nearly throwing her water glass in surprise. Corwin laughed at her expense, and Dani joined in. "Jilly doesn't make it any easier, huh?"

"She doesn't bother me."

"Really? Most people would be at least a little scared."

"It was scary before I got to know her, but only because I was afraid someone had actually broken in."

"Why doesn't she scare you?"

"After everything I've been through, people scare me more than ghosts. Besides, the raven in the barn is way freakier." She laughed and refilled her water glass.

"Raven?" Dani froze. *There goes my stupid mouth, getting ahead of my brain again.* "There aren't a lot of those around. Is its mate here, too? I'd love to see." Dani took a long drink. *He just thinks I don't like birds. It's fine.*

"No mate that I've seen."

"Can we go see it before it's too dark?"

"I guess. It's just a bird." She hoped he wouldn't see past her attempt at a poker face. Her heart beat faster as she led him outside. Knowing what she knew now about Jake, she had no desire to face the raven she was certain shared a connection with him. She stopped just outside the barn, gesturing inside. "Every time I've come in, he's been there. Sometimes back by the work bench." Corwin stepped past her into the barn, eyes sweeping the rafters.

"Hey there, little guy." Dani peeked around the corner. Corwin had located the raven perched on the workbench. "Are you looking to start a project? I'm not sure how you'll hold the hammer, buddy, but I believe in you." Dani grinned in spite of herself. *He's a dork.* She stepped into the barn.

"You could always offer to help." Corwin and the raven turned to look at her at the same time. Corwin was smiling. The raven only glared at her for a moment before launching himself into the air. He flew at her, talons aimed for her face. Dani squawked and stepped backwards. She tripped over the partially exposed, crumbling foundation. She saw Corwin running toward her. The raven had flown past, but she knew he'd be swooping back around. She flipped onto her knees, scrambling back to her feet just in time to see the raven, talons extended, just a few yards away and closing fast. Corwin pushed her forward. For a moment, she pushed back, away from the raven.

"The house. Go." He pushed harder and she submitted to his direction, ducking to avoid the raven. Between the raven's forward momentum and their speed in the opposite direction, Dani figured they just might make it to the back door before the raven could. *The steps,* she thought, *we're almost there.* She reached for the doorknob when they were still a few steps away. As she leaned for the door, Dani lost track of her feet. Her toe stubbed into the bottom stair and she was falling. The concrete stair caught her just under the left kneecap. She felt Corwin's arm wrap around her, his hand under her left arm. He pulled her forward and up as he pushed the door open with his right hand. Dani scrambled to get her feet under her, succeeding only in scraping her legs across more hard surfaces and probably making Corwin's job harder. He dropped her onto the entryway floor and Dani pulled her feet toward her, out of his way as he slammed the door shut. The raven crashed into the window at the top of the door and fell to the stairs with a thump. Corwin and Dani didn't move. Corwin stared out the window at the raven, still braced against the back door as if to keep them safe. Dani lay on her back on the floor, feet still drawn to her butt. Both breathed heavily.

"Is he dead?"

"Huh?" Corwin turned to her, dazed.

"The raven. Is he dead?"

Corwin turned back to the window. "It still hasn't moved. If it's not dead it'll have one hell of a headache." They stayed like that a few minutes longer. Dani's knee began to ache and her back objected to her awkward position. She sat up slowly and drew her jeans up. No blood. She let her pant leg slide back down.

"I think I need a drink."

"Make it two." Corwin offered his hand and helped her stand up slowly. "You okay?"

"Yeah. My legs will just be pretty." She hobbled into the kitchen, Corwin's hand on her back for support. "Okay, so maybe my knee is a little tender." She pulled down two plastic cups and shifted to the cabinet where she'd tucked her whiskey away from her parents' prying eyes. As she poured them each a generous drink, she heard her freezer drawer slide open. She turned to find Corwin holding a bag of frozen corn.

"How about you head to the couch and I'll bring the drinks and what apparently serves as ice around here." Dani considered arguing, but figured she'd struggle to carry their drinks without spilling them right now. She hobbled to the couch and settled in, groaning as she sank her exhausted body into the softness. Corwin carried their drinks in carefully, frozen corn sandwiched between the cups. He set their drinks on the coffee table and slowly lifted her foot onto the corner of it. Dani leaned back and closed her eyes as he gently arranged the corn on her knee. She didn't bother to open them when she felt him sit down. His hand bumped hers. When she didn't move, she felt him nestle the bottom of a cup into it. She opened her eyes and took it, taking a long swig.

Corwin sniffed the cup. "Lighter fluid?"

"Basically. Drink up. We've earned it. We just survived a homicidal bird attack after doing physical labor." She took another sip of her whiskey.

"When in Rome," Corwin said, lifting his glass. He took a tentative sip and winced. "I'll certainly have hair on my chest. And if I drink all of this, I won't be driving home." Still, he took another, bigger drink. They drank in silence for a bit. As the shock wore off, Dani began to feel pains in nearly every part of her body. Each drink lifted her closer to not caring. Her head was delightfully fuzzy when Corwin spoke again.

"Wanna tell me about the raven?" His eyes met hers and she knew she couldn't lie to him. Not when he'd just saved her from serious bodily harm.

"No. But I will." He chuckled, but his face grew serious as she filled in the gaps she'd left in her earlier story. How she'd come to find the gun and letter. The way the raven had looked at her. "I think he was trying to get me to see his version of the story before she could. I think they coexist here, somehow."

"You don't believe his story, or at least he knows you've heard hers, so he attacked you. Makes a weird kind of sense. But I still don't understand why he'd stay here."

Dani drank, thinking about this. "I guess he could have hidden out around here if he didn't want to leave his family. Or didn't know where to go. But I can't believe no one would have ever found him."

"No chance he offed himself?"

"I guess it's possible. I doubt Papa would have wanted to admit that." She sat up, wincing, and reached for her computer. "If he did die, there should be an obituary somewhere. Why didn't I think of that before?" She tried several versions of his name. Jake Lind. Jacob Lind. Ja* Lind. Nothing. She experimented with adding 1973 to the search. Still nothing. "There's nothing. It's like he never existed."

"Weird. What about Jilly?"

"Let's see." She searched for Jilly Lind 1973 and the screen filled with links to news articles. "Bingo." She clicked on a link to her obituary. Corwin leaned closer to read over her shoulder. The name at the top, next to a head and shoulders shot of Jilly, sent a shock through Dani.

"Of course," she whispered. "Corwin, why didn't we think of that? Her married name wasn't Lind. She was married to my uncle." She clicked open another tab and searched again. "Jake Foxer 1973," Dani said as she typed and struck the enter key.

"Your last name is Foxer?"

"No. Yes. It will be again," Dani shook her head, wanting to focus. *We are so close to figuring this out.* Corwin cocked his head, but said nothing, skimming through search results over her shoulder. She clicked on some and they skimmed them in silence before shifting to another. There were articles about Jilly's murder, of course. Jake was listed as a person of interest in those articles. Later, the articles shifted to a focus on Jake as a missing person. Finally, his name was listed in his mother's obituary before it faded from history altogether. Satisfied that she'd found the basics, though a few articles remained open in other tabs for closer examination, Dani leaned back.

"He really did disappear." Corwin's voice almost made the statement into a question.

"It wouldn't have been smart to stick around after you murdered your wife. But if he actually left, how do you explain the raven?"

"I said he disappeared. Not that he left. Wouldn't it make sense that he died here if he's sticking around in the form of that raven? Maybe even in the barn?"

"Okay, but then how come nobody found the body?"

"Clearly somebody did. Law enforcement cover-up? Family secret? Animals got to him first?" Something about his suggestions started a nagging feeling in the back of Dani's mind. She pushed at it, but the feeling wouldn't go away and wouldn't come fully into the light.

"You're on to something, but I'm not sure what."

~ 10 ~

Dani didn't sleep well that night. Dreams of ravens and small brown pills kept her on edge and awakening periodically. The next morning, she struggled to get out of bed and resolved to crawl right back in after chores. She threw feed to the calves, scratching the foreheads of the braver ones. She went to the finishing barn next, trying to put off the long walk to the boars. Thankfully, nothing was needed in the finishing barn and she was quickly on her way to the boars with her heavy buckets. Water splashed her legs as she poured it into the first boar's pan. He didn't come up as he usually did, asking for scratches and slurping water while she dumped in his feed. Dani called to him, but he stayed in the back corner of his pen. He was standing up and she was sure he was fine, but still. His behavior was odd and she didn't like it. She crawled over the fence and approached slowly. When she got close the boar turned his head to look at her and Dani shrieked. A tail hung from his mouth while he chewed slowly. A snake, by the looks of what remained of it.

"Dude. Not cool." She stomped to the fence and climbed back out. "People think goats will eat anything. They really need to meet pigs." She was halfway through caring for the other boar before it hit her. *Pigs will eat anything.* She texted the phrase to Corwin.

"Most people just say good morning." Dani smiled. Then another text, "Did they have pigs?"

"I don't know, but even if they didn't, I'd bet somebody around here did. Now to figure out how he died."

With no clear path to that answer, Dani settled for going back inside and working on the house. She was far too awake now to go back to bed. She carried boxes to her truck for Dad to go through, clearing the top of the stairs. There was still room in the pickup bed when she was done, so she settled in to go through more boxes. Army men, more children's books, Dani fell into an easy rhythm. There were boxes of baby blankets, tiny knit booties, and a rattle that looked ancient. Jilly had been a dreamer, for sure. Had she really wanted children with Jake? Or was she preparing herself for a life after him?

Dani made her way through at least a dozen boxes before deciding she needed a break. She rinsed the dust from her hands and swept a washrag over her face and through her hair. Satisfied that she was clean enough to sit on the couch, Dani sat down to grade assignments and respond to student questions. It was an adjustment, but she found herself enjoying the freedom of online teaching. With assignments pre-scheduled, instructional videos already posted, and asynchronous discussions, she could work whenever she wanted. It was faster this way, she discovered. More work ahead of time, but then so much less during the semester. She answered a question about a due date, barely restraining herself from typing "Look at the syllabus." A quick email to check on a student who hadn't engaged in class yet. She laughed as she scored discussion board posts. College freshmen were unique creatures and she had missed them. One young man had responded to a classmate's discussion board post by simply writing "Okay, dude." Another found a way to tie her wiener dog into every single bit of writing she did. She texted Kat and they exchanged their first student stories of the semester.

"So....how was Corwin?"

"We got a lot done. He was super helpful. And sort of saved me from a homicidal raven."

"And then he slept over? Because that should be the only reason I didn't hear from you until now. Wait. Did you say homicidal raven?" Dani laughed. "Story, please." A second later, her phone was ringing, a video call from Kat.

Dani filled Kat in and showed off the blooming bruises on her legs.

"Dude! I'm telling Corwin to go easier on his dates."

"Still not a date, Kat. And I prefer bruises to being impaled by a raven's claws. I bet they carry all kinds of germs." She shuddered.

"Okay, but you're convinced the raven is Jake?"

"Yeah, I think so. Corwin agrees, which helps me feel a little less crazy. You?"

"It makes sense. Somehow you have to figure out what happened to Jake. That's the key to this whole thing. If you find out what happened to him, you'll know which story is true. But if you do, you may be releasing your woman in white."

"Huh? You mean Jilly?"

"Yes." Kat sighed. "We've been over this. She's a woman in white. So if you help her resolve the issue with Jake, she'll probably leave. She'll be at peace."

"Right. I didn't exactly go do the kind of research you wanted. But I've been reading *The Woman in White*. Does that count?"

"Wilkie Collins? No. It does not count. But it does have the best first line of a novel ever. 'This is the story of what a Woman's patience can endure,'" said Kat.

"And what a Man's resolution can achieve,'" Dani finished. "The perfect first line. I know some of what Jilly endured. I just don't know yet what man's resolution we're talking about. I know what Jake's resolution achieved, but if somebody helped him out of this world, that's the resolution I'm more interested in."

"I'd say somebody definitely helped him disappear, even if they didn't help him leave, exactly. What about the person in the barn?"

"I don't think so. That person was young, short. I don't see how a preteen, teenager at best, could kill him and dispose of him. He's a big guy. Was a big guy."

"Maybe they had help?"

"Maybe. I wonder if Jilly knows who it was. I'll ask her later."

Dani heard a knock at Kat's door. "Oh, shit. I forgot. Frank's here."

"Frank?"

"Wind turbine engineer." Another knock at the door. "If he turns out to be worth it, I'll tell you all about him."

"Not holding my breath. Love you."

"Love you, too."

Dani stood and stretched. She was caught up enough on teaching to ignore it for the moment. Boxes for her father's perusal needed taken up to his place, but he'd be out working right now anyway. Might as well wait for tonight and get some supper she didn't have to cook herself. If the dumpster had arrived, she'd work on that, but the window for drop off didn't start for another hour, and even then it was a three hour window. She poured herself another cup of coffee and stood at the window, sweating in the summer heat but enjoying the coffee's warmth anyway. Birds flitted from trees to grass and back again. A bee flew in lazy circles around the flowers under the window. She took another drink of coffee and turned toward the stairs. Only two options left: talk to Jilly or read. First one, then the other, she decided.

In Jilly's room, Dani leaned against the wall, still sipping her coffee. Her legs hurt, so she opted not to attempt to lower herself to the floor. She knew she might regret that when the dizziness hit, but she just couldn't bear to bend her swollen knee. One more sip of coffee and then Dani took a deep breath. Coffee cup clenched between both hands. Time to see what Jilly knew.

"Okay, Jilly, I'm so close to knowing everything about what happened here. So I can help you. Just one more thing, I think." She hesitated. This answer could change everything. Was she ready? "Jilly, who saw Jake murder you?" Dani braced herself for the nausea, the spinning feeling, the vision changes. Nothing happened. "Jilly?" A thumping sound. *So she's here. She doesn't know?* Dani finished her coffee. *What now?* Jilly was her only real link to the past. Her father either didn't know or wasn't willing to talk. Her mother had to have known Jake and Jilly, but seemed otherwise oblivious. *But why didn't she tell me about Jake and Jilly? Mom. That's my next move.* She pushed herself away from the wall and hobbled to her bedroom. She needed time to think about how to approach her mother. She picked up *The Woman in White* and went back downstairs. She settled onto the couch with her book, a bag of frozen corn on her knee, and her laptop within reach. She was fully immersed in Victorian England, far from the humid Midwest, when her phone vibrated. It took a moment for her brain to register the sound.

A text from a number she didn't have saved was previewed on the lock screen. "You thought you could get away that easy? I know where you are now. You'll never see me coming. Unless you want to be reasonable and take me back. I don't want to live in the cou…" Dani didn't move. Of course he'd gotten a new number. Of course blocking him hadn't been the victory she'd imagined. He didn't know where she was, though. That much she was confident of. If he had bought her old car, then he'd been looking around her parents' house, though, and he was getting too close for comfort. Eventually he'd see her driving up there or them driving down here. And eventually would be soon. She texted Kat. She needed someone to bounce her options off of. She listed them for Kat.

Option 1: Ignore him. Delete and block.

Option 2: Ignore him. Wait to see what he says next.

Option 3: Respond. Call his bluff and invite him to come over. See if he actually knows where I am.

Option 4: Respond. Tell him to go kick rocks.

Kat's response came quickly. "Option 5: Restraining order."

Dani hadn't considered that option. "How do I do that?"

"You save everything. Every text." *Oops, already messed that up.* "You call the cops and you show them the messages and your divorce decree. They'll help you from there."

"He's not going to go away, is he?" She felt a sinking in her chest. "Not even with a restraining order."

"I doubt it. But we won't know unless we try."

Dani decided not to tell Kat that she'd already deleted his other messages. It wouldn't take long for him to fill up her phone with new evidence, she was sure. Then she'd do as Kat suggested.

Unable to sink back into London, Dani closed her book. She snagged her laptop and tried to do some teaching work. Her mind wouldn't focus. She snapped the laptop shut and stared ahead, seeing nothing. Dani fought the urge to curl up and go to sleep. It came on strong when she was overwhelmed. She considered whiskey, her backup option when sleep wouldn't come, but she knew she might need a clear head later. Mama. She couldn't drive up there, for fear of leading him to her new home, but she could call. Mama would no doubt be working in the garden, but she'd answer.

Mama picked up on the third ring. "Hang on." Dani heard fumbling. "Can you hear me?"

"Yes, Mama. Can you hear me?" More fumbling and mumbled, muffled curses.

"Oh, there it is. Now can you hear me?"

"Always could, Mama. Can you hear me?"

"Yes. Sorry, I'm picking beans. I've got you on speaker now, though."

"Good. I've been working around the house and wondered if you knew a few things."

"Well, I doubt it, honey, but I can try. Your dad would know, though."

"I know, but he's busy," *and he wouldn't tell me anyway,* "and he doesn't know how to use speakerphone."

Mama laughed. "True enough. What can I help you with, baby?"

"I found this old metal barnyard set. Little animals and fences and such. Do you know anything about it?" Dani had intentionally chosen a soft question that she didn't really care about to break the ice.

"I don't, but I'd bet it was one of Jake's toys from when he was little. It sounds like the kind of thing he would have had."

"Do you think Papa will mind if I keep it?"

"Not at all. I can't imagine he'd have any use for it."

"Thanks." Dani took a deep breath. "Do you remember that rock I mentioned to Papa? I texted you about it, too. The one with JML 1973 etched in it?"

"Yes, but I don't remember a text." *Does Mom sound on edge?*

"Now that I know about Jake and Jilly, can you tell me what the rock is about?" Dani bit her lip, praying she wasn't overstepping and that Mama would tell her something, at least. The silence on the other end went on forever.

Finally, Mama sighed. "I suppose so. I don't know much about it except that your father is the one who put it there. He used her maiden name initials. I'm not sure why. Maybe it was an accident. He was young and missing his brother and Jilly. He and Jilly were close. He helped her around the house and farm a lot. I didn't know them well, but your father says Jake wasn't the most stable or hard working."

Papa put it there? Why? "What all did Papa do for them?"

"Little home repairs, evening chores almost every day, he'd help them work lambs and pigs, lots of things. I remember he helped Jilly plant her garden once."

"Do you know why he put the rock where he did?" *Where she was murdered?*

"Not really. He said it was under her window, in her favorite flowers. I guess I just thought she liked looking down there. He just wanted to remember her, honey, and to make sure other people did, too."

Then why didn't I ever know about her? "Right." Dani hoped she'd kept the sarcasm out of her voice. *Papa knew where she died. Papa did evening chores. Papa saw her die. Papa was the watcher in the barn.*

"I need to go get another bucket. These beans are going like crazy this year. Did you have any other questions?"

"No. Thanks, Mama."

"Sure, dear. But like I said, your father would know more."

You have no idea. She flipped idly through her phone after they hung up. So Papa clearly knew where she died. How? She ticked through the options in her head. He could have been the watcher in the barn. He could have been called by his brother to help clear up the mess. He could have witnessed the investigation afterward. She had a hard time believing that Jake would have called Liam, at the ripe old age of 11, to help move a body, or that her father would have helped if he had. Equally hard was picturing Grandma allowing little Liam to watch the investigation. She'd never really known her, but the stories she'd heard painted Grandma as a strict, sheltering figure who hadn't wanted to let her little boys grow up. *Might have been part of the problem there, Grandma.*

A knock at the front door made Dani sit bolt upright, nearly dropping her phone. *Who the fuck would be here in the middle of the day?* He was her first thought. But then, he probably wouldn't knock, at least not without trying the door first, which wasn't locked. *Why don't I lock my doors? Stupid.* The knocking sounded again. Dani eased herself onto the floor. Her knee protested, but she gritted her teeth and scooted slowly on her bottom toward the living room window. It offered a view of the front door. She pushed the curtain clearly donated by her maternal grandmother aside just a fraction. *Who the fuck wears a suit in this weather?* She dropped the curtain back into place as the man knocked again. *Door to door salesmen don't exist anymore, do they? Jehovah's Witness? Is there even a Hall nearby?* The man knocked again, paired with a deep, "Hello?" Dani pulled herself up off the floor and hobbled to the door. *Whoever it is, it's not him, so I can probably handle it.*

She pulled the door open just a crack. "Can I help you?"

"I hope so. Are you Dani?"

"No. Who are you?" The man looked flustered.

"Oh, I. Are you sure?"

Dani bit back a laugh. "It depends who's asking."

"Me. Oh, umm, I'm Eric. From Finch's office." Dani said nothing. "Your attorney?"

"Eric. What is it that you do?"

He beamed. "I'm a paralegal."

"Are you new?"

"Yes. How did you–I'm messing this up, aren't I?"

"A little. Now, why are you here, Eric?"

"Well, we only have thirty days to reverse your divorce and your husband said he would be out of town, so Finch asked me to bring the papers to you." He looked around uncertainly. "Is there somewhere we can get these signed?"

Dani froze, pretty sure her jaw was on the floor. "Did he give you this address?"

"I, uh, no. He said for what he's paying us, we could find it ourselves."

Dani took a deep breath. "Eric. I need you to listen carefully. Do not, for any reason, share this address with him. Do you understand?"

"But he. How will you? You're not going to live together?" Eric's eyebrows were knit together as he tried to process the scene in front of him.

"No. And I'm not signing your papers. I do not want to reverse the divorce and I do not want to hear another word about it." She pushed the door closed. *Good grief. What wouldn't he do?* She turned around, back to the door, and let herself slide down, anxiety ebbing.

"Do you need my card?" Eric was shouting to be heard through the door and Dani winced at the sudden sound.

"No, Eric. I'm not changing my mind." Maybe it was time for a restraining order. But she didn't have enough evidence for a restraining order yet and she wasn't sure it was worth pursuing if she did. So far, all he'd done was lie to a church lady and cruise by her parents' house. He was bigger than her, but with her newly acquired gun skills, he wasn't much of a threat. Not that she wanted to shoot him, exactly. Sure, she'd fantasized about it, but all that paperwork and the investigation. Not worth it. But just the sight of the gun was likely to scare his city boy butt away from her for good.

Dani waited for her heart rate to decrease, taking slow, deep breaths. She was feeling a bit lightheaded. Probably time for lunch. She never was good at remembering to eat meals, which left her a little confused as to her weight. Once she felt calm again, Dani reached behind her to the doorknob, using it to help her get up while putting as little weight on her sore knee as possible. She moved slowly to the kitchen and snagged a loaf of bread on her way past the counter. She made her sandwich in the fridge so that she wouldn't have to shuffle back and forth to it to grab ingredients. Once it was assembled, she tossed the bread to the counter as gently as possible and shuffled back to the couch. Time to eat and nap. Her body and brain had had enough for one day.

It was growing dark when Dani woke. She was sweaty and her mouth was dry. It took her a moment to identify the buzzing sound. Her phone. Where was it? Dani sat up, feeling the pain in her knee bloom back to life. The buzzing stopped, then started again a few seconds later. Someone was calling. Dani felt her pockets. Not there. She couldn't see it on the couch, so she plunged her hand behind the cushions, trying to pinpoint the direction of the sound. Finally, her fingers brushed the phone case and she tugged it free. She swiped to answer before her brain had quite processed that the phone said "No Caller ID."

"Where are you?" Dani snapped to attention. "I know you can hear me. I can hear you breathing. You sound scared. Tell me where you are and I'll come keep you safe." Dani pulled the phone from her ear slowly and pushed the red button to hang up. She stared at the phone and, for a brief moment, considered smashing it to bits. It buzzed again. No caller id. She threw it to the other end of the couch and hobbled to the kitchen. She needed a drink.

Dani sipped the whiskey slowly, consciously ignoring the buzzing sound coming from the couch. A few sips was all it took to steady her. She made her way back to the couch and scooped up her phone. She swiped to ignore the call and started a new message group with Kat and Corwin. Everyone was on the same page anyway. She told them about the lawyer and his phone call. It was too much to process alone, especially when she could feel him closing in.

"Can Corwin see your location? He should. He's closer than I am."

"No. Sharing now." Dani turned on location sharing to Corwin's number. "Headed out to chore."

"Check in when you're done, please." She liked how Corwin added the "please" to make it seem like a request.

Between the pain in her legs and hiding every time a car approached, chores took longer than usual. Her phone buzzed regularly in her pocket. She didn't bother to check. If it was anyone other than him, she'd find out when she got back inside. If it was him, she didn't need to see or answer anyway. She approached the finishing barn last.

"Anika, so help me, get back in your pen or I will find a use for this pistol." The slim white pig stared blankly at her. "You think I'm kidding? Okay. I'm not kidding, but I also won't shoot you. Then Papa would shoot me. So just get back in your pen so we can all live, 'kay?" Anika seemed to think about this before walking toward Dani and nuzzling her boot. "Or stay out and starve. Whatever." Dani slammed the door of the finishing barn, feeling irrationally guilty for yelling at the pig. She walked slowly back toward the house, enjoying the cooler temperatures and the technicolor sky created by the setting sun. When she reached the open-sided shed from which someone had watched Jilly's murder, she stopped. Had her father really witnessed his brother turn into a criminal from here? She went inside, standing about where she thought the light had been coming from that night. Sure enough, she had a clear view of the rock that marked where Jilly had drawn her last breath.

"What were you doing here, Dad? Why did you just watch? Were you scared? Of course you were scared. You were eleven. And your brother was a monster." Dani leaned against the shed wall, staring at the house. Maybe it wasn't fair to judge her father. He was so young and the events so horrible. *But he let her die.* She knew that he would probably have died, too, if he had intervened. Or at least he wouldn't have been able to stop his brother. And despite the secrets, Dani still loved her father. *But I need answers. And there's only one person left to ask.* Dani stood up straight, squared her shoulders, and walked with as little limping as possible. Her phone buzzed in her pocket. She ignored it. Jake had some explaining to do.

Dani reached a hand out to the corner pole of the barn, steadying herself as she stepped over the crumbling foundation exposed by the missing door. She braced herself for a raven's attack. This time, she would not duck. She would not scramble. If she was right and the raven was Jake, he wouldn't hurt her. Not when he heard what she had to say. It took a moment for her eyes to adjust to the darkened interior of the barn. It would have been the perfect moment for Jake to attack, but he didn't. Dani frowned, confused.

"Jake? Are you here?" A fluttering of wings from the back of the barn. "I realized something today, Jake." She took a careful step into the barn. "I don't know your side of things." She let her left hand trail along the wall to guide and steady her as she moved slowly, carefully, quietly toward the work bench. "Jilly was able to show me her memories. Can you do that? Can you show me what happened, Jake?" A throaty squawk this time. *Great. Now I need to speak bird.*

She was close enough to see him now. He stretched his wings out and lowered his head. She reached slowly to her shoulder holster and snapped the flap free. Hand on the pistol grip, she stepped closer.

"I just want to know your side of things, Jake. But I will shoot you if you fly at me again." The raven didn't move, locked in a staring match with Dani. Finally, he dipped his head lower and raised his wings as if to fly. Dani drew and pointed the pistol at him. She flicked the safety off, but kept her finger on the trigger guard. "Not kidding." The raven froze. "Chill out and show me your side or we'll find out what happens when you get killed a second time." The raven cocked his head, then pulled his wings into his body. His head stayed low, but Dani decided it was good enough. She didn't holster her weapon, but she relaxed a bit, aiming it at the floor instead of at Jake.

"So how does this work with you? I just had to ask Jilly a question and she could show me the answer. I'll try that first, unless you want to pick now to tell me you can talk." She waited, half hoping he could talk. No luck. "Okay, here goes. Jake, what did you do after you killed Jilly?"

Darkness descended quickly. Dani looked around, wondering if a storm had kicked up, but there was no wind. Red tinged the edges of her vision. An anger she couldn't explain welled up inside her. Her hands tightened on the gun. Jake's memories were going to be a rougher ride than Jilly's. She turned back to the work bench, but Jake was gone. She turned around slowly, scanning her limited field of vision for him. Finally, a squawk led her to the barn door. She followed the raven out of the barn and to the corner of the house. She watched Jake slam Jilly's head onto the rock again. She felt sick, but the anger was gradually lessening, replaced by panic. Jake set Jilly's head down gently, smoothing her hair back. It was almost tender. Dani felt the panic in her throat now. *He certainly handles panic better than rage.*

Jake stood, outwardly calm despite what Dani knew he felt. He looked down at himself. Dani could see the blood spattered on his clothes, arms, face. When he looked back up, his eyes were wide. The raven hopped along the ground behind Jake, Dani trailing behind, as they made the short walk back to the barn. Jake walked to the center of the opening, as if the walls and door were still there. *Maybe they were back then,* Dani thought. She stopped at the corner pole again, waiting. Jake stalked back to the work bench. He placed both hands on it, hunched over. Suddenly, he dropped to one knee and reached beneath the bench. *The gun.* Dani aimed her own gun at his back. Irrational, she knew, but she wasn't entirely certain how this all worked and she wasn't taking any chances. Jake spun, gun held loosely in one hand, dangling toward the floor. He paced to the center of the barn before turning back to the work bench. He removed the clip, checked the weapon over, and slammed it back home. When he turned again, shock registered briefly on his face before a deep scowl took its place.

Dani turned to see what he was looking at. "Papa." She felt her breath leave her.

"Liam. What are you doing here? You should be home in bed by now."

Liam said nothing. He just stood, staring at his older brother.

"What? Liam. Buddy. What?" Jake's voice was growing slowly more panicked. He took a step toward his brother. "It's me, Liam. You can tell me anything." He reached toward his brother, as if to comfort him. That's when Liam saw the gun. He made a small sound and stepped backward, mouth open.

"Oh, buddy, no. This isn't," Jake waved at the gun dismissively, "I was just checking it. You should always check your guns." He was talking fast now, nearly incomprehensible. Liam had stopped moving.

"I saw you." It was so quiet that Dani thought she had imagined it. Jake and Liam were still. She wondered if the memory had frozen or glitched somehow. Then, she saw Jake's eyes widen, blinking fast.

"You what? What did you see?" His voice was soft and low. He stepped closer to Liam, who stood a little taller.

"I saw you kill Jilly. I saw you. I saw you." He was screaming now. Angry. "She was good."

"She was a whore, Liam. She wasn't who she said she was. She was going to leave me. Everybody leaves, Liam. Everybody. She was in my dreams, keeping me from sleeping. Her face was bloody, gone. She hated me, Liam, so she haunted me. She drove me crazy so she could leave." He was gesturing wildly, gun still in hand.

Liam's eyes followed the gun, but he didn't back down. "She wasn't leaving. She was packing to move with you. You were making her leave us. She loves it here. She loves us. It's you, Jake. You're the crazy one. You came back all wrong. Everybody knows it. You're the one who left. It's your fault.

You killed her." He stepped toward Jake, hands balled into fists at his sides.

Jake aimed the gun on instinct. Dani could feel that, somehow. Still, she took her finger off the trigger guard, ready to squeeze to protect her father. *He lives*, she reminded herself, and moved her finger off the trigger. Liam studied Jake.

"You really are crazy," he whispered. "You gonna kill me, too? Find a way to get rid of both of us?" Before Jake could answer, Liam lunged at him, keeping himself low to the ground. Jake fired, the bullet going far above and behind Liam. He hit Jake just above the knees, surprise and leverage bringing Jake down into the dust. Liam crawled over him, reaching for the gun. Jake twisted onto his stomach, knocking Liam off of him. As Jake pulled his knees under him, Liam gripped the barrel of the pistol. Jake pulled back, aiming the pistol squarely at Liam's chest. A well-aimed kick dropped Jake back to his stomach and Liam was able to push the barrel up, aiming it at the sky as Jake rolled over.

"You little shit," Jake growled. Liam had two hands on the gun now. He knelt next to Jake, trying to twist the gun from his grasp. Jake had the size advantage, though, and he knew it. He sat up, dragging Liam forward through the dirt. "Come here, little man. Let me show you how this works." He jerked the gun from Liam's hands and aimed it again as he rose to his feet. "Stand up, now, I don't want to shoot a man while he's down."

Liam's eyes scanned the barn. He stayed on his knees.

"I said stand up." Jake motioned with the gun.

Liam put his hands up at shoulder height, as if assuring Jake that he meant no harm. Dani looked around the barn. He was up to something, but what? Slowly, Liam shifted his weight and placed his right foot on the ground.

"I'll stand up. But I don't think you'll like it when I do. I think you better just put that gun away now, before somebody gets hurt." He spoke calmly. Far more calmly than Dani imagined she would have at age eleven with a gun in her face. He was definitely up to something.

Jake laughed. "Oh, really, big man? What are you gonna do? Didn't your daddy ever teach you to respect the man with the gun?"

"There's a lot my daddy didn't teach me," Liam said. "But one thing I know for sure. Not every man with a gun deserves respect." He pushed off hard with his right foot, diving to his left. Jake fired and Liam yelped, but Dani couldn't tell if he'd been hit or just frightened by the sound. He kept moving, grabbing at something on the wall. A hay hook. He gripped the handle and swung back in the direction of his big brother. He missed, but it was enough to make Jake jump back. Liam pressed forward, wielding his newfound weapon.

"I hate to break it to you, kid, but gun beats hay hook any day of the week." Liam grunted and moved forward, swinging again. He caught Jake's shirt this time, ripping it across his stomach. "So close," Jake taunted, dancing backward. He'd relaxed now, enjoying the game. He held the gun loosely in one hand. It was no longer aimed at Liam, just an extension of his arm, which was high in the air, mocking his little brother. The dance continued. Liam striking, ineffectually, Jake dancing backward in a half circle around the barn.

Then, Dani saw it. Her father did have a plan. He was, ever so slowly, backing Jake up to the work bench. *What are you doing?* She let her gun drop to her side. Two more swings of the hay hook and Jake's back collided with the work bench. Dani felt fear jump into her throat again, but it was quickly quelled, taken over by a sense of amusement.

"Oh, little brother's got me pinned. What ever will I do?" Jake laughed. It was a musical sound, and Dani imagined that it had been wonderful to hear before he'd lost his mind to the war.

Liam gritted his teeth and raised the hay hook. Jake's eyes widened and he tried to lower the gun, but Liam was too close. The hook caught Jake in the forearm of his gun hand and stuck there. Jake screamed, part pain, but mostly Dani felt the intense rage rise again. Liam tugged at the hook, trying to free it for another blow. Jake jerked his arm away, gripped the gun in both hands as best he could, and took aim at Liam once again.

"You messed up, little brother." Liam's eyes narrowed. He stepped forward, the tip of the gun barrel touching his chest now.

"Do it, then." His jaw was tight, but his hands were relaxed. He watched Jake's finger move from the guard to the trigger. Liam moved like lightning. He shoved the gun to the side, toward Jake's wounded arm. Jake squeezed, but the shot struck the barn wall. Liam kicked at Jake's feet, distracting him. The gun was his now, and he took aim and fired. There was no pause, no time for thinking things through. Jake was on the floor now. One single bullet through his forehead. Liam stood stock still, gun aimed at the place where his brother had been standing. His eyes drifted to his brother's body on the floor. He dropped the gun, then, and knelt beside his brother.

"Jake?" He shook him. "Jake. I'm sorry. It wasn't you. I know it wasn't you. But Jilly. You killed her, Jake, for nothing. For things you imagined. It wasn't real. None of it was real. You tried to kill me, Jake. I'm your brother. Why? Why did you make me kill you?" He was sobbing now. A raven hopped over to him, perched on Jake's chest. Liam sat back on his heels. "Jake?" The bird cocked his head and squawked. Liam scrambled backwards, tears still streaming down his face. He sat against the barn wall like that for a while. The raven stayed, watching him. Then it flew to the work bench, picking at the underside of the shelf. Dani knew it was Jake, trying to show Liam the letter. Liam didn't follow the bird. He just stared at his brother's body.

"I'm sorry, Jake, but I need to get rid of you. I wish it didn't have to be this way." He stood, limping a little. Dani saw the blood on the back of his jeans. The shot must have caught him in the calf. There wasn't much blood. A graze wound, maybe. She watched as Liam built a fire in the can outside the barn. He wrenched the hay hook from Jake's arm and tossed it in. Then, he undressed Jake, tossing his clothes into the burn can one article at a time. It was ceremonial, almost reverent. Liam left the barn for a few minutes. Dani stood watch. He went to the shed and returned with a tarp. He laid it out next to his brother and carefully rolled him onto it, then rolled his body with the tarp to create a tube. A piece of twine secured the end closest to the body. Liam pulled from the other end. Dani and the raven followed. He drug the body far from the house, all the way to the finishing barn. Back then, it had just been an open hog lot. Dani saw the fence and hogs as if they were a mist overlaying the current structure. He paused, unlatched a ghostly gate, then drug his load through. He untied the end and unrolled the tarp. Liam watched for a moment as the curious boars nudged at the body. He turned away after he saw the first one take a bite.

The memory ended abruptly. Dani was standing next to the finishing barn in the pitch black. Her phone was buzzing nonstop. She leaned over the railing of the nearest pen and puked.

Dani stood, hands braced on the top of the fence, staring west at the dark horizon. She was only vaguely aware of her phone's buzzing. She'd need to answer Corwin and Kat soon, before they called the cops. *Do I need the cops?* Dani pulled out her phone and fired off a text to Kat and Corwin.

"I'm fine. Jake showed me his side of things and it was a lot. I'll call you later to fill you in. Need a minute to process right now."

"Don't scare us like that!" Kat was a little upset.

"Glad you're okay. Better be a good story." Okay, so Corwin might be upset, too. They'd both be fine when they heard all that had happened. Or at least whatever she decided to share.

It was pitch black and Dani felt cold despite the summer heat. She wrapped her arms around herself and stumbled back to the house. Inside, she poured herself some whiskey, in desperate need of its painful heat. She drank deeply. A thump sounded from upstairs.

"I'm okay, Jilly." She refilled her whiskey and retreated to the couch. Kat and Corwin wouldn't be satisfied with her brief text for long. She popped open her computer and plugged her phone into it to charge. She needed to decide how much to tell her friends before she called them. *What is the statute of limitations on murder?* A quick search yielded the answer she was afraid of. There was no time limit on murder charges. Not unless you lived in Connecticut, and her papa was a long ways from the Constitution State. She couldn't tell them. Not unless she decided he should turn himself in. *Papa's what, sixty now? This was fifty years ago. He killed a monster and he's toed the line ever since.* Her phone buzzed, disrupting her thoughts. A group Face Time. She answered, still debating what to tell them.

"Hey, guys. I'm so sorry."

"What on earth happened?" Kat's face was free of makeup and her hair tightly contained in a head wrap.

"No date to distract you tonight?"

"Frank wasn't so great after all. Don't change the subject."

"Who's Frank?" Corwin smirked, clearly willing to help her change the subject now that he had visual proof that Dani was okay.

"Well he's nobody now. I washed my hair today, if that tells you anything." Kat paused, realizing what was happening. "Stop helping her."

Corwin laughed. "She's fine, Kat. Look at her. She's inside, she's got her whiskey, and I'm sure she's learned to lock her doors by now." He glared at her through the screen.

Dani smiled. "The doors are wide open for visitors, but the rest is true."

"Go lock your doors right now," Kat demanded. Dani rolled her eyes, but unplugged her phone and hobbled to the front door. She flipped the deadbolt. She hesitated at the back door, looking toward the barn where the raven lived. *Is he still there, or is he gone now that he told me his side of the story?* She flipped the lock. She'd check on Jake tomorrow.

"Okay. Doors are locked." Dani eased back on the couch, kicking her leg up to allow her swollen knee to relax.

"Good. Now, story time." Corwin's tone was gentle, but Dani could feel his impatience.

"Right. Chores took longer than usual because somebody drug me up concrete stairs yesterday–"

"To save you from a homicidal bird. You're welcome."

"Anyway, I stopped at the shed that I saw the lights coming from while Jilly died and I decided Jake owed me some answers. So I walked straight into the barn and asked him for them."

"And that worked?" Kat was wide eyed.

"After I pulled my gun on him it seemed to." Dani laughed. "Y'all are so serious."

"Forgive me. It's not every day my best friend takes her life into her own hands by approaching the raven that tried to kill her."

"What she said," Corwin agreed.

"He showed me his side of that night. He felt so panicked. I really think he had PTSD, guys. I almost felt sorry for him for a minute."

"And then what, you saw him bash his wife's head in?" Corwin had a way of phrasing things that made Dani laugh despite the grim subject.

"Well, yes, something like that. Then he went to the barn. I think he was trying to figure out what to do next. He got his gun. I wonder if he was going to kill himself."

"But he didn't?"

"Not exactly. The person who watched the murder came in before he could." She paused. *Do I tell them? What if they think I should turn him in? I probably should anyway.*

"Well? Who was it? Anybody you know?" Kat was clearly out of patience.

"It was Papa. He would have been eleven. He was so little, but he confronted Jake. They fought and Jake pointed the gun at him, but Papa just attacked him anyway. He shot Papa, just a graze on the leg, but still." Dani's mind was racing even faster than her mouth, trying to decide how much to tell them.

"Whoa. You're tellin' me an eleven year old took on a full grown adult?" Dani smiled at Corwin's slight drawl.

"Even better. He won. That scrappy little kid attacked his brother, got the gun, and shot him." Dani clapped her hand over her mouth. She'd gotten so excited to tell them the story. *What now?* The video was silent.

"So he was a minor," Kat said.

"Acting in self defense," Corwin added. "No court in the world would convict him. Do we know what happened to the body?"

Dani nodded. "Pigs." She grimaced, remembering watching the boar take that first bite. "Effective, but not pretty."

"I can't imagine living with that all those years. He did the right thing, hundred percent."

"For sure," Kat said. "Somebody had to stop him. Jake wasn't gonna just change his ways."

"I can't tell if you're just trying to make me feel better or telling the truth. Either way, thanks."

"Oh, sweetheart, I don't humor people. You could turn him in if you really wanted to, but let's walk this through." Corwin's voice turned professorial. "You call the cops and tell them your dad murdered his brother in 1973. Great. They're gonna ask you how you know."

"I," Dani thought, "Well, I just do. I suspect him? Someone told me?"

"And if the cops were out at Jilly's murder scene the next day, why didn't they find Jake? We all know pigs are good, but they're not *that* good."

"Maybe he went back and hid the bigger pieces the next morning?" Dani shrugged.

"You really think they're gonna send an officer out to arrest your dad, or even just investigate, an almost fifty year old murder on 'I suspect' and 'Maybe?'"

"Well I can't really tell them a ghost showed me."

"No, and without that you ain't got any idea who did what, do you?"

"I, well, no. I guess not."

"Do you even know Jake was telling you the truth?" Dani could see that Kat was liking this line of thinking.

"Okay, okay. I see your point. I know this, but I don't. The authorities wouldn't do anything."

The three sat in silence again. Finally, Dani smiled. "Thanks, guys. Now we wait to see if Jilly and Jake leave, huh?"

"And if Corwin ever goes on a date with that chick from the coffee shop," Kat grinned.

"Oh my gosh, right?" Corwin rolled his eyes and Dani was relieved to feel like she had a normal friendship again. Mystery solved and the hardest parts of her life, she hoped, over with, Dani relaxed into the friendly banter.

~ 11 ~

Dani rose early the next morning. Her legs still ached, but the pain wasn't as sharp as before. She tossed aside the sweaty sheets and stretched. After doing chores as quickly as possible, she poured herself some coffee in a travel mug and headed up to Jilly's room. The dumpster had finally been dropped off the day before and positioned under the western windows.

"Okay, Jilly. Today, we clean this up." There was no answer from Jilly. Dani took a sip of coffee before setting the cup on the floor and picking up the scoop shovel borrowed from the shed. She scooped up a load of plaster and tossed it out the open window, watching it crash into the dumpster. Slowly, Jilly's room began to feel clean again. Dani paused for coffee periodically and looked for signs of Jilly. It still felt cooler in the room than in the rest of the house, but Dani knew it was likely wishful thinking. As she sipped her coffee, she texted Kat and Corwin.

"Is it crazy that I kind of miss Jilly? No sign of her this morning." She tucked her phone away. She knew neither of them would be up at 7am. As she cleared more of the room, Dani began to think about next steps. She'd need to get someone to help her hang drywall, then mud and tape. Paint, trim, flooring. Did she want to build in a closet? She'd need to deep clean between mudding and taping and all of the other finishing. *What color do I want my walls?* Dani stood, leaning on the shovel handle. She tried to imagine the room in its finished state. A cool grey blue on the walls, white trim, and a barn wood feature wall. She stepped off the space needed for a bed. *Plenty of room left for a closet along the wall. It can even be a walk-in.* She'd need to consult with someone who actually knew a bit about remodeling, but she was excited for her future bedroom.

Dani only had a few shovelfuls left when her phone buzzed. *No Caller ID.* "Not today, Satan." She shoved the phone back into her pocket and finished the plaster removal from Jilly's room. She cleared the old carpet from the room across from her own next. She propped the shovel against the wall in the hallway and began shifting boxes from the center bedroom to the tiny one. She didn't want to get bogged down in going through the boxes today, but if she moved them, she could get the plaster in the center bedroom down. Box by box, Dani shifted Jilly's dreams and keepsakes into the smaller bedroom. She'd go through them soon, she promised herself, but for now she just wanted to get the messy part of the remodel done.

She was nearing the last of the boxes when her phone buzzed. Corwin had texted. He didn't tell her she was crazy for missing Jilly, although he hadn't known her long enough yet, she reasoned. He also offered to come help her, and Dani decided she really would like company after all that had happened. He'd be there in half an hour, he said. She smiled, slid her phone in her pocket, and moved the remaining boxes. She stepped back into Jilly's room for a break.

"I hope you'll like what I do here, Jilly. It should have been yours still, but I promise I'll take good care of it." She stood there, waiting for a thump, a flash, even a bit of dizziness. But Jilly was gone.

A scuffing sound on the stairs startled Dani from her thoughts. She ducked inside the bedroom, hand on her holstered pistol.

"Dani?" She stood upright, breathing a sigh of relief.

"Hey, Corwin. You scared me."

"Good. You were supposed to lock your doors."

"Oh. Right. I must have forgotten after chores. It'll take a bit to get in the habit."

"Fair enough. No harm, no foul. I won't even tell Kat."

"How generous of you." Dani rolled her eyes. "I am armed, so it's not like I was defenseless."

Corwin made a face. "I am unconvinced that you would have shot an intruder."

"But the intruder wouldn't know that."

"Uh-huh." Corwin turned to survey the changes to the house. "Since we're going to agree to disagree on this one, let's talk shop. What's our plan today?"

Dani walked Corwin through what she'd already done. Soon, they were at work knocking plaster down in the center bedroom. Corwin was on the ladder, getting the ceiling started in one corner while Dani worked in the opposite corner on the walls. Once they had the bulk of the plaster down, they would remove the trim boards and finish it up before throwing the plaster out the window and into the dumpster. Corwin put some red dirt country music on his phone and they worked without talking. Dani's phone buzzed once, just Kat assuring her that it wasn't weird to miss Jilly.

By the time Corwin called for a water break, they were both covered in sweat and plaster dust. They stood in the kitchen, guzzling water and fanning themselves.

"You okay after last night?"

Dani cocked her head and stared out the window at the barn. "I wonder if the raven is still there."

"Good answer." Dani turned to face Corwin, smiling.

"I honestly don't know. It's one thing to know your dad is quiet and mysterious. It's another thing entirely to know he's hiding something like that from everyone in his life. As awful as it is, I know he did the right thing. And I think you're right. No one would probably even charge him, much less convict him of anything. I just need time to process."

Corwin nodded. "Fair enough. I'm here if you ever need to process out loud. Or just work yourself to death while your brain sorts it out."

Dani clinked her water glass against his. "Cheers to that. I prefer to let my brain do the work without me."

They'd nearly braced themselves for the return to work upstairs when Dani's phone buzzed.

"Who's the man whore?" Dani's body froze even as her heart and mind raced.

"Dani? You okay?"

"Did you lock the door?" She stared at the phone.

"What's going–"

"Did you lock the door?" She was louder this time, and there was an edge to her voice.

"Yes, of course. I locked it when I came in. You wanna fill me in on the details here?"

Dani shoved the phone at Corwin. "Son of a–" He looked up at Dani. "So he's here or drove by at least. Want me to call the cops?"

"Not yet. He might be guessing. He always accused me of cheating. He never stops with one text. There will be more."

"In the meantime, let's get where we have the advantage. The doors are locked down here. Up we go."

"Won't we just get trapped upstairs if he gets in?" Dani was moving upstairs anyway, trusting Corwin's instincts even as she questioned him.

"We'll be able to track his movements easier from above. We'll know when or if he gets here. And if he does get in, which he won't, we'll be shooting from above if we want or climbing out a window if we don't. Whatever way you slice it, we've got the advantage if we've got the high ground."

They went to Jilly's room, since it offered the advantage of views of both the road and the driveway. Dani's phone buzzed in Corwin's hand.

"I saw his car in your driveway. Are you really moving on that fast, Dani? Did I mean nothing to you?"

"First of all, it's a truck," Corwin said.

"He never was one for attention to detail. It doesn't necessarily mean he wasn't here. Just wait. The texts will come faster now. They always speed up when I don't answer."

They sat down, backs against the south wall, keeping close watch out the northern and western windows. The phone buzzed and then buzzed again before Corwin could even read the first message.

"Here we go," Dani grimaced.

"You're my world, Dani. Come back. Please. Or I can move in. Whatever you want." Corwin looked up.

"Prince Charming, eh?"

"Keep reading." Dani didn't meet Corwin's eyes.

"I know we could make this work if you weren't such a bitch." Corwin's eyebrows raised. "You'd rather whore around than stay home and be a good wife."

"Didn't peg you as the whoring type."

"Depends who you ask, I guess. I was pretty sure I'd only slept with one man, but what do I know?" Dani laughed.

The texts came quickly, but rather than scare her, Dani found herself laughing at them with Corwin. There were no more details about Corwin or his truck, so they decided that he must have been guessing. Still, they made sandwiches for lunch and ate them in Jilly's room, keeping watch. They took turns fetching a box of Jilly's keepsakes to go through, so that they weren't totally unproductive. Mostly, though, they talked, and Dani thought how nice it was to have an in-person friend again.

It was nearing supper time when Dani and Corwin finished sorting through Jilly's boxes. Most items were in a pile for her father to go through, though they'd taken the liberty of tossing molding crayons into the dumpster.

"Well, I don't think he's showing up today. I need to get chores done either way. Wanna help?" Dani felt pretty certain that Corwin wasn't going to leave anyway, so she figured he might as well be useful.

"You bet. I also want to see if our raven friend is still around. I've got a hunch he's gone, but I want to be sure. Just let me call my folks real quick to make sure they can chore for me."

Corwin stepped over to the window and dialed a number on his phone. "Hey, Dad. Got a situation here." He paused and looked at Dani. She nodded. "Kat's friend Dani, the one I'm helping today, her crazy ex is around and threatening. I'm thinking I oughta sleep on her couch tonight." There was a long pause while he listened to his dad. "Yup. I agree, Dad. But we both know they won't do anything tonight." He listened again. "Thanks, Dad. Appreciate it."

He turned back to Dani. "All set. Dad thinks we oughta go to the cops. Can't say I disagree, but we'll let you sleep on it and deal with that in the morning."

Dani nodded, grateful that she wouldn't have to face the police today, at least. "I hate for you to sleep on the couch, but I've only got the one bed."

"And contrary to your ex's beliefs, you're not the whoring type. I know. The couch will be just fine, I promise."

"Okay, then. Let's get chores done and get back inside. Hopefully I can scrounge up some sheets for you, at least."

On their way out to chore, Corwin and Dani stopped by the barn. They entered cautiously, aware that, if the raven was still there, it might attack. Corwin went first, peeking around the corner and then edging into the barn, back to the wall. Dani leaned around the corner pole. A quick scan revealed no raven. She stared at the workbench, where her father had gained the advantage over Jake. No wonder he hadn't been happy to hear about it. No doubt the writing on it was Jake's. Corwin continued to explore the barn, checking rafters and examining the few things left inside the barn.

"He seems to be gone." Dani's eyes were still fixed on the workbench. The fight played over and over again in her head.

"Seems like it." Corwin pulled the shepherd's crook down from its spot on the wall. He turned back to Dani. "You alright?"

"Yeah, it's just. I watched Papa," her voice trailed off.

Corwin approached. "Right. But remember that you only saw what Jake wanted you to see. We don't know how much he can manipulate those memories. Whatever your dad did, he did because he had to." He touched Dani's shoulder and she met his gaze. "If he hadn't, you wouldn't be here."

"I know. I just need time to adjust. This isn't the kind of thing I ever anticipated learning about my family."

"Don't think anyone does. Why don't you use this to support that knee while you show me what chores need done?" He guided her gently away from the scene of the fight.

They shared the load of the chores, for which Dani was grateful. The cane was helpful in easing the pain, not that Dani intended to admit that to Corwin. He laughed at Anika's antics, which Dani informed him was only possible because he hadn't put up with them daily. When all was taken care of, they re-entered the house and locked the door.

Dani's phone buzzed on the counter where they'd left it. They both jumped, then laughed. The texts from him had stopped before chores. She didn't realize she was holding her breath until she scooped up the phone to find a message from Kat and let out a deep sigh.

"Kat wants to know if you're still here." Dani paused, blushing. "Sort of."

Corwin chuckled. "What did she actually say?"

"'Is Corwin staying tonight? You've only got one bed. Make sure you share nice.' And then she sent some emojis." Corwin raised an eyebrow. Dani rolled her eyes. "Really? Okay, fine. She sent the eggplant and the water splashes." Corwin laughed loudly.

Dani rolled her eyes and pulled down a cup and the whiskey bottle. She raised an eyebrow questioningly at Corwin, who managed to stop laughing long enough to confirm that he'd like a glass of whiskey.

"I'm glad to see the idea of sleeping with me is so funny," Dani commented sarcastically.

Corwin struggled to sober himself, taking a sip of whiskey before replying. "Oh, it's not that. You're an attractive heifer," he jabbed her in the ribs at this and they both laughed as she playfully slapped him back. "But I hardly know you. Hey!" He sprang back from Dani's renewed assault.

Dani video called Kat. "Give me one good reason not to kill him." Dani did her best to keep a straight face.

"So you're not sharing the bed?" Corwin cackled in the background. Dani rolled her eyes.

"He called me a heifer."

"Corwin, did you call her a heifer?" Kat's tone reminded Dani of a mother refereeing a fight between her children while trying not to laugh.

"I would never." Corwin had pulled his face into the closest approximation of innocence he could manage, but his face was still red from laughing.

"Why don't you two go lock yourselves in Dani's room until you can work this out."

"But Moooom," Dani whined. They all laughed. Dani sipped her whiskey, enjoying the feeling of laughter and ease.

"Seriously, though, where are we at with the threatening ex?" Dani filled Kat in on his vague threats and lack of actual appearance.

"Corwin is sleeping on the *couch* tonight just to be safe. Doors are locked. Cops in the morning. He'll give up soon. Right?"

Kat tilted her head. "I mean, he doesn't tend to stick with things for long. Especially if something else catches his attention. I'd still call the police, though. You don't want to risk him finding you before he loses interest. I know Corwin has you all trained up on that gun now, but still, I would rather it didn't come to that."

"Ditto," Corwin said.

Dani laughed. "The nineties called. They want their catch phrase back. But I agree. I promise I'll follow through with the cops."

Kat turned the subject to teaching, then, and the three spent the night chatting and laughing. Corwin and Dani moved easily around the kitchen, making supper together while Dani's phone charged, propped up on the counter to include Kat. Finally, drunk on more whiskey and laughter than she'd had for a long time, Dani said goodnight to Kat and Corwin and headed up the stairs. She brushed her teeth and stopped in the hall, staring into Jilly's room. She tiptoed down the hall, acutely aware that Corwin could probably hear her every move. She stopped in Jilly's doorway. The only light was from a yellowed, fading bulb on the power line pole and the moon. The strange combination gave the room a yellow grey glow.

"I'll miss you if you're gone, Jilly," she whispered, "but I'm glad you've found closure. I hope you'll like what I do with your house. I hope you'll be able to see it." She waited, half hoping for a sign that someone had been listening. The room was quiet, though, and no telltale flashes broke the darkness of the night. Jilly was well and truly gone.

Dani moved slowly to her own room. When she reached to remove her shirt, she realized she was sorely in need of a shower. No sponge bath would do tonight. *Dang, I bet Corwin would like one, too.* She put her shirt back on and pulled clean clothes from her drawers, then darted downstairs to offer him the use of the shower, even if she couldn't offer him any clean clothes.

"Hey," she said, cautiously poking her head into his makeshift bedroom. "I just realized I need a shower and thought I'd make sure you knew you were welcome to it, too. I know you don't have any extra clothes, but still. If you want."

Corwin looked down at his clothes, clearly coming to the same realization she had. "A shower would be nice. Clean clothes would be even better. Wonder if I have something stashed in my truck. I'll go look while you grab me a towel?" Dani nodded and he headed out the back door.

Dani had just dug a towel and washcloth out of the bathroom cabinet when Corwin returned from his truck and re-locked the door. "Pay dirt," he said, holding up a white t-shirt and a pair of well-worn jeans.

"Awesome. You go first." Dani handed him his towel and washcloth and walked to the kitchen, trying not to wonder if he'd found any extra underwear. She felt awkward just standing, waiting for him to shower, so she went upstairs to retrieve her book and perched on the edge of the kitchen counter reading. She was engrossed in the heroine's escape from the asylum when Corwin emerged from the bathroom. Dani didn't notice and Corwin approached quietly. He leaned against the counter next to her.

"What ya readin'?"

Dani started, let out a strangled scream, and smacked Corwin with the thick book before realizing what was happening and devolving into laughter. "You scared me."

"I kind of got that impression. Shower's all yours." Corwin headed toward the couch. "I made sure I left some hot water."

Dani was keenly aware of Corwin's presence in the house as she stripped and turned the water on. She took a deep breath, willing herself not to think about her last shower before moving back home. She stepped into the shower stall and slid the door mostly shut, leaving it open just a crack. She took a deep breath, wondering why the presence of a man she trusted in her house made her so sensitive to the memories. Hair soaked, she grabbed the shampoo. She stared at the ceiling as she massaged the shampoo in. The memory of his sudden entry into the shower, his hands hard and cold, bending her unwilling body to his desires made her lose her breath. She braced herself against the wall. Her breath came in deep, ragged gasps as she fought the panic. *He's not here. No one is going to touch you. He's. Not. Here.* Finally, she felt her heart return to its slow, steady beat and her breath came easier. She finished rinsing her hair, gave her body a cursory scrub, and stepped out. She dried and dressed quickly, wanting to escape the bathroom as quickly as possible.

Dani walked quietly to the stairs, flicking off lights on the way. She could hear soft snoring from the living room and smiled. Corwin was settled in, then. When her head found her pillow, Dani slipped into sleep quickly. Her mind was alive with the events of recent weeks, though, and she dreamed.

A tall, slim woman in a flowing white dress stood next to Jilly's rock. She looked down, as if reading the inscription. Her dress blew in the wind. She moved as if in slow motion, looking up from the rock and walking around the house to the barn. The woman in white stared straight ahead. She knew where she was going. When she reached the barn, she walked inside without hesitating. The raven waited inside on the workbench. The woman held out her hand. The raven flitted to her, gripping her fingers with its feet. Their eyes met and neither moved for a long moment. Then the woman turned and walked out of the barn with the raven still perched on her hand. She walked west and faded from sight.

~ 12 ~

Dani woke slowly. She stretched and threw the sheet off. The smell of coffee drifted up the stairs along with the sound of clinking pans. She put on a sports bra, t-shirt, and jeans before heading down to see what Corwin was making for breakfast.

"I could get used to this," she said, watching him pour what appeared to be pancake batter into a pan.

Corwin laughed. "Don't," he said. "I'm not usually a morning person. And it would be one hell of a commute to come make you breakfast every morning."

"Details, details," Dani said dismissively. She ran a hand through her tangled hair and leaned against the counter next to the stove. "No more messages from him. At least not yet." She poured herself a cup of coffee and sipped slowly. "I'll go do morning chores real quick while you finish making breakfast." She saw Corwin open his mouth to object and rushed on. "You'll be right here, and if I'm not back in, say, twenty minutes, you can panic. Besides, you can see most of my chore paths from the kitchen window, and you'll definitely hear if he pulls in the drive."

"Fine." Corwin looked supremely unhappy. "But I'm checking on you in ten minutes."

"I can't be done in ten."

"I know. But I'll be done with this in ten. Take it or leave it."

Dani huffed, but set her cup down and tugged on her boots. "Be right back, ya jerk."

"Be safe," Corwin called after her as the door slammed.

Despite her relaxed state and assertion that she'd be fine, Dani caught herself checking the road frequently as she rushed through chores. A tractor chugged along the road, passed by a truck with buckets rattling in the back. Dani started at the sight of a dark sedan, but relaxed when she recognized the driver as her parents' elderly neighbor, probably on her way to have her hair done. She shook her head, trying to clear it of fear and caution. Anika was out again, and Dani was feeling generous, so she took the time to coax her back into her pen. She scratched a few curious noses before heading for the door. *I could get used to this, too*, she thought. She pushed the door open and turned to latch it against Anika's escapades.

"So you're a farmer again, huh?"

Dani froze. She felt cold, despite a heat index in the 90s already. *If I don't look, it won't be real.* She studied the rusty hook, still not moving.

"What, you don't want to see me?"

Deep breath. Try for your phone. Dani lifted her eyes along the rough wooden door. Slowly, she turned around and looked up to meet his gaze. *Of course this is the day I leave my gun inside. Stupid.* Dani slipped her hands into her back pockets, trying to effect a relaxed, casual stance while activating her phone and trying desperately to remember how to dial 911 without having to look at the screen.

"Don't I get a kiss? Or at least a hug? It's been awhile, honey." He took a step toward her, and Dani instinctively backed up until she was pressed against the door. He frowned. "Still a cold bitch, I see. We'll have to remedy that." He took another step and Dani decided she didn't care if he knew she was calling 911. She needed help now. When she pulled the phone from her pocket, it began to vibrate. She glanced at the screen. Corwin.

"I have to answer this. It's someone checking on me. You don't want anyone coming to check on me, do you? If I don't answer, they will." Dani did her best to act as if she didn't care either way.

He studied her for a few long seconds before nodding. "Answer it. On speaker. Convince her you're okay so we can talk, honey."

Dani answered and pressed the speaker icon. "Corwin, I'm almost done. Just put Anika back in."

"Okay, this made more batter than I thought, so I figured I'd call so I could keep cooking and still check on you. You sure you're alright?"

Dani glanced at him quickly, gauging how suspicious he would be. "I'm good. But be careful if you go to your truck for anything. That raven we thought had left the barn is back." His face grew cloudy and Dani knew the conversation was about to be over. "It'll probably be fine, but I'd hate for you to get attacked again." He made a fierce gesture and Dani knew she had to hang up and hope Corwin had understood. "Be back in soon." She hung up without a goodbye, hoping it would add to the oddness of the call and bring Corwin outside, preferably armed.

"A raven? Is that code for me?"

"No. There was a raven in the barn," Dani nodded toward it. "It attacked us the other day. That's why I'm limping a bit. Banged my knee on the steps trying to get away from him."

"Proof."

Dani stood, confused. "What?"

"Prove it. Show me your knee."

Dani leaned down slowly and tugged the jeans up gingerly, revealing bruises all along the shin and, finally, the swollen purple knee. "Good enough for you?" She couldn't keep the sarcasm from her voice, dangerous though she knew it was.

He stepped closer, his eyes nearly black. "Don't take that tone with me, dear. You know how it gets me going."

It took conscious effort not to react. Dani made a point to roll her jeans back down even more slowly than she'd pulled them up. She raised back up slowly, meeting his eyes. "So sorry." She glared, daring him to challenge her insincere apology.

"Well, then, let's talk about us. If you want to live here," he gestured at the house and disgust flickered across his face, "I suppose I can move in. But not for long. We can do better than this place. Or you can do the smart thing for once in your life and move in with me. I've got a nice little apartment in Kaxe. Perfect for just the two of us, until we start a family."

Dani felt bile rise in her throat. *Corwin might not come. What can I do?* She thought quickly, mind flicking over the items close at hand, but careful not to shift her eyes to reveal her thoughts. The auger that delivered feed to the pigs inside the finishing barn was just a few feet to her right. Leaning against it was a length of rebar, used to help unclog the auger when dampness caused clumps in the feed.

She took a step slightly forward and to her right. "It's so beautiful here, though. Have you looked around? I mean really looked?" She took another step toward the auger. "If you look down that way you can see the trees along the crik." *Almost there.* "And this land is all ours. All the way down to the crik." She placed her hand on the auger and slowly slid her hand down, praying he wouldn't notice her groping for the rebar and that it was where she'd remembered.

"'Crik?' Really? You are such a hick sometimes. It's disgusting."

Her hand closed on the rebar. *Finally.* "Creek. Sorry. The property goes all the way down to the creek." She took a half step backwards and pulled the rebar up as he looked away, still examining the property lines. She gripped the rebar with both hands, like a baseball bat. "And I'd really like you to get off of this property. Now."

Startled, he spun around. "What did you say to me?" The sight of the rebar seemed only to anger him further. "Put that down. You won't hurt me. Do you hear me? You will not hurt me."

The sight of her ex-husband, unarmed, trying to command her while she stood with a weapon that could, at the very least, knock him down struck Dani as funny. She smiled, trying to fight the laughter. It bubbled over, though, and she found herself laughing out loud.

"You think this is a joke? This is not funny, Dani. You put that down and pack your things. You're going home with me."

"How? How exactly do you think you're going to make me do any of that?"

He advanced on her then. Angry. His arms were up, ready to grab at the rebar. Despite her advantage as the only armed party, Dani felt fear wrap itself around her insides. She braced herself, ready to strike if he didn't stop.

"I have had enough of this, Dani. You are coming with me." Dani thought he sounded something like a wounded animal. He was in range now, and he wasn't stopping. Dani gripped the rebar hard and swung. She felt shockwaves vibrate up the rebar into her hands. She heard a crunching sound coming from his ribs. He made another animal sound and flopped to the ground. It was less dignified than Dani had expected, somehow. And it was odd, seeing him look weak. She stood, rebar raised, waiting to see if he would get back up. But he stayed down, whimpering.

"You. Bitch," he finally bit out between gasps of pain.

"Should I call you an ambulance?"

"So you can tell the police your side and get me thrown in jail until they figure out you're a lying bitch? No." His anger was rising again and seemed to be helping to mask his pain. He was attempting to rise to his feet when Dani heard a sound behind her and whirled, prepared to strike.

"Easy, tiger," Corwin said, hands raised, her gun in one of them. "I came to help, but I see you've got it handled. Need me to dial the cops while you watch him?"

"Is this the guy you've been whoring with? Don't lie to me. I know he made you breakfast." He was up now, but hunched over, a protective arm over his ribs.

"That I did, but I don't think we've got enough for you. Guess you'll have to leave." Corwin looked around, spotting Dani's old blue car parked in a ditch up the road. "Ah, there's your car. I can help you to it or I can call the cops. Your choice." He made eye contact with Dani, who nodded.

"I'd recommend leaving. If I see you or hear from you again, or any of my family or friends do, you'll get a visit from the cops. I've got plenty of evidence for a restraining order, maybe more." Dani stepped to the side, opening up a path for him to walk toward the road.

"This isn't over," he growled as he passed her.

"Oh, it is. If you decide to show up again, I'll have my gun strapped to me and I will shoot first, then call the police. It won't go well for you."

He mumbled something under his breath, but he continued toward his car. Dani felt a strange pang, watching him climb into her old blue car and drive away.

Dani and Corwin stood silently, watching until the car was well out of sight.

"Dani?" Corwin's voice was soft and soothing. "He's gone, and I don't think he'll be back." Corwin wrapped his free hand around the rebar, just above Dani's. He pulled gently and Dani released the rebar, hands falling to her sides. Corwin threw the rebar to the ground and looped his arm around Dani just as she began to crumple. "Hey, hey, I got you. You did it. You got rid of him."

"I did it." Dani stood upright again, but stayed inside Corwin's supportive embrace. She looked at Corwin, eyes wide. "He's gone."

"And you didn't even need your gun or anyone's help. You're a badass."

Dani smiled. "How about some pancakes as my reward?"

"All the pancakes you want."

~ 13 ~

"Finally," Dani collapsed dramatically in the middle of Jilly's room.

"You really do hate painting, don't you?" Corwin laughed at her.

"Always has," her mother said from across the room.

"I like the results," Dani said, "but good grief it's annoying to get there." She sat up to admire the grey blue walls and white trim. "Thanks for the help, guys."

"Any time," her father's baritone echoed from the doorway around the empty room. "It's nice to see it alive again. It's nice to see you happy again."

"Think we can save the original floors?" Dani was uncomfortable with her father's rare display of emotion.

"I bet we can. Liam, you think this spot will sand out?" Corwin gestured to a dark spot near a window where moisture had undoubtedly come in at some point.

Her father walked over to examine it more closely, picking at it with his forefinger. "It's not soft, so it probably would. At worst, you'd just have a dark spot here, but I think it would still look alright."

"I've got a floor sander at my place you can borrow. I finally got mine all done."

"Thanks," Dani grinned at him. "If you do the sanding I'll even feed you."

"Unlikely," Corwin shot back, "but I'll do it anyway. You'd get distracted halfway through and ruin it."

"Children, children," Liam put both hands out, as if to keep them from fighting. "Play nice or I'll put you both in time out."

Dani laughed. She hadn't told her father that she knew his secret, but he'd relaxed in recent weeks. He knew. And somehow, it freed him.

Painting completed, they headed downstairs for water and snacks. Her mother handed out cookies. She and Liam leaned against the counters to eat while Corwin and Dani collapsed on the floor. They rested in silence for a moment.

"Corwin," her mother said, "how's that girl? The one you were seeing?" Dani rolled her eyes. *Every time you see him, Mom? Really?*

"You mean Ally? I'm still seeing her. She's amazing. Doesn't make me do all the manual labor." Dani smacked him at this.

"Dani," Liam said, "I will still send you to time out." He was grinning as he said it, though, so Dani risked one more slap to Corwin's shoulder before settling back down to finish her cookie.

"Really, though, I think she's a keeper. Dani likes her." He looked to her for support.

"I do. She's smart and sarcastic and tough. She's basically as close to me as Corwin could get." She smiled sweetly at Corwin, who glared back at her.

"On second thought, maybe I don't like her so much."

"Oh, you two," Mama said, annoyed. "I just don't understand–"

"Why you're not together," Dani and Corwin said in unison. Liam laughed and quickly covered with an unconvincing cough.

"I'm not ready, Mama. I just beat the crap out of my ex a month ago. And even if I was ready, Corwin's the brother you never gave me. Let it go."

"And I just watched her beat a man with a length of rebar. I'm out." Corwin raised his hands in mock fear.

"Give me one good reason," Dani raised a fist.

Later, snacks consumed and mess cleaned up for the moment, Dani waved as her mother and father pulled out of the drive and headed back to their place.

"They're right, ya know." Dani turned at the sound of Corwin's voice. He stood, supplies in hand, ready to walk to his truck.

"About what? The colors? I know, but I love purple."

"No. Well, yes. For the record, I think you'll regret a purple bathroom. About us. We'd do well together."

Dani cocked her head. "Even without that attraction spark?"

"It would be better with the spark. No doubt. That's why I'm with Ally now. There's a spark and a good fit. But if that doesn't work out, if we're both 40 and single, I'm coming back for you." He kissed her on the cheek.

Dani put her hands on her hips. "40 and single, huh? Sounds like a plan. But don't mess it up with Ally. I like her. She's good for you."

After Corwin was gone and chores were done, Dani felt truly alone in the old house. She relished the feeling. She was on her own when she wanted to be and it was glorious. She poured a glass of whiskey and grabbed *The Woman in White*. She texted Kat, alerting her to her 40 year engagement to Corwin. *She'll be thrilled.* Kat replied immediately, ready to plan the wedding that was still fourteen years away and unlikely at best.

"Take a breath, Kat. It's not happening."

Kat, however, had no plans to take a breath. So, Dani went with Plan B. "You know what, I bet Corwin would love to talk about this with you."

Smiling, she sunk into the couch and sent Corwin a quick text that just read, "Sorry."

"Dani, what did you do?" A few seconds later, his follow up text told her he'd heard from Kat. "Oh, Dani. Why? She's never going to let this go."

"Sorry!" Dani responded. "Muting my phone for the night. Enjoy!"

Content, Dani opened to her bookmark, wondering if she would find herself in the story of a woman who endured the worst that men had to offer and the man who persisted in his love for her even when it cost him everything.

www.ingramcontent.com/pod-product-compliance
Lightning Source LLC
LaVergne TN
LVHW041809060526
838201LV00046B/1182